JIM DANDY
A JUSTICE SECURITY NOVEL
By
T. M. Bilderback

Connect With The Author
Other Works By T. M. Bilderback

Chapter 1

THE DAY WAS ON THE cusp of twilight...those slim moments between the time when the sun dips below the horizon and the time when full darkness reigns. Daytime animals were beginning to settle into their hiding places to sleep the night away. Most birds were already in their roosts, but a few brave robins were tilting their heads at the soil, hoping for a last minute snack. A lone cricket began his lonely chirping, waiting for the chorus to join him later. Two bats swooped and fluttered in the air, gulping down mosquitoes.

"Nothing pershonal, Mr. Mosquito. Just one bloodshucker to another," said Michael Brandon, too drunk to realize that he was speaking out loud. He was seated on the big hill that overlooked his small town. Fifty-two, thinning hair turning more grey than its normal blonde, and the start of a spare tire around his middle, Brandon was the local branch manager for Second Fidelity Bank, Tucker's Corner, Oregon – the only branch in Harney County. And his options had just run out.

"Nothing a little good nooshe won't fixsh...sinsh I'm just hanging around," he said, again out loud. This remark made him chuckle to himself. "Yep, she gonna mish me when I'm gone..."

"No, she won't," said the pale guy. "That's why she divorced you, and married that other guy. She won't give a second thought to you."

Brandon snickered, the laugh actually a self-derisive chuckle. "Yeah, you're prob'ly right," said Brandon, slurring his words. "Looks like you're the only fren' I got, buddy boy."

The pale guy nodded. "Sure. Sure I am. You just want to make sure that gun is ready to go when you are."

"I think itsh ready," said Brandon. "I can see bulletsh in the sillen...sil...*cylinder*."

"Good!" exclaimed the pale guy. "Now, all you have to do is put the end of the barrel into your mouth, point it up, and pull the trigger."

Brandon tried to remember the pale guy's name, but couldn't. "But what if I want to use a noosh inshtead?" He took another pull from the whiskey bottle while he waited for the pale guy to answer.

When Brandon looked around after taking a drink, the pale guy had disappeared.

"Jusht my luck," he said to himself.

Brandon fell back onto the late summer grass along the hill, and looked up at the sky. The first star had popped into sight, and Brandon made a wish.

"Shtar light, shtar bright," he started. He didn't finish. His voice faded out gradually, as if it were being heard as it moved away.

Brandon's wish was simple. He wished that he'd never seen those bank files.

He wasn't supposed to find them. They were well hidden, and he wouldn't have found them if the balances hadn't been off. The hidden files were controlled by his boss, Luther Utley. Utley had been on vacation for the last two weeks, and those hidden files were obviously brief storage areas for money.

Laundered money.

And now Michael Brandon was a man sentenced to death for knowing something he wasn't supposed to know. What was frustrating about it was the fact that he knew where the money was *from*, but not where it was *going*. He knew the offshore bank and account number that the money would be passed to, and he knew the money was from an account used by Esteban Fernandez...but he didn't know who owned the offshore account.

Now, he would never know.

But someone else would.

Brandon had made three copies of the files and information on three different jump drives. He had mailed one of the drives to his ex-wife, one to himself at a mail drop, and one to a friend he had met years ago. This friend had his own security business in the city. He figured the one at the mail drop he could forget about. He wouldn't be around to claim it, and the padded envelope would just be tossed aside when the rent on the mail drop was used up. He hoped that his ex-wife, Angela Harriman, would survive the mailing, but the people that were assigned to kill him would probably figure he would mail it to her, so Brandon had probably signed Angela's death warrant the minute he dropped the envelope into the mail. He had done a little soul-searching, wondering if he should warn her, but he found that his conscience was clear on that. If Angie was killed because of that mailing, he figured the cheating bitch had gotten what she deserved. Karma was a bitch.

The third copy, however...that was his beyond-the-grave revenge on whoever had ordered his death. No one in town, not even his ex-wife, knew about his friendship with...

"Hey, are you gonna use that gun, or just play with it?" The pale guy was back. "It's not your dick, you know."

"Whyn't you jus' shut the fuggup?" Brandon took another long pull from the bottle.

"Looks like you're too late, Michael," said the pale guy, who was actually a shadow of himself. "See you on the other side."

Two men in off-the-rack business suits had come to a stop on either side of him.

The one on the left had a light smile on his face. "Michael Brandon."

"Whaddaya want?" Brandon was drunk enough to be belligerent, but too drunk to stand up and do something about it.

"We just wanted to say goodbye," said the man on the left, as the man on the right shot Brandon in the head.

ANGELA HARRIMAN ARRIVED home from work frustrated. She had tried once again to get a man she worked with at the warehouse in trouble, but it had backfired on her. Her butt was still sore from the ass-chewing she had gotten from the Operations Manager.

She slammed her purse down on the kitchen counter. Her husband, Allen, wasn't home yet. She began thumbing through the mail. One of the things that had come in the mail was a brown padded envelope. There was no return address, but Angela recognized her ex-husband's writing on the front.

What does that asshole want? she thought to herself.

She tore open the padded envelope and looked inside. All that was inside was a jump drive. She shook it out into her palm and looked at it. Just then, Angela's cell phone rang. She put the jump drive down on the counter, along with the torn-open envelope, and scrambled to get her phone out of her purse. She finally got it out of her purse, and answered the call.

"Hello?"

"Angela Harriman?"

"Yes?"

"This is Agent Smith with the FBI. May we come by and talk to you?"

"The FBI?" A chill went down her spine. "May I ask what's going on?"

"We'd rather tell you in person, if you don't mind."

Angela had puzzlement in her voice when she responded. "Sure. I guess it's okay. Come on by."

"We'll be there in just a couple of minutes. Thank you."

Angela disconnected, then looked at her phone with irritation. *Now what?* She just had time to hit the bathroom before the FBI arrived.

When the knock came at the door, Angela opened it to see two men in off-the-rack business suits. One had a small wallet open, displaying what appeared to be a badge and an FBI ID card.

"Hello, Mrs. Harriman. I'm Agent Smith, and this is Agent Johnson. May we come in?"

Angela pushed the door wide. "Come on in."

The two men came inside the house and looked around the living room.

Agent Smith turned to Angela. "Nice house."

"Thank you. Would you gentlemen like some coffee? I was just about to make some."

"That's very generous. Thanks."

The men followed Angela into the kitchen. Angela began rinsing the coffee carafe, then filling it with water.

"What's this about, Agent Smith?"

Angela finished preparing the coffee pot, and turned it on.

"Mrs. Harriman, do you know the whereabouts of your ex-husband?"

"Michael? At the bank, I would guess. Why? Has he done something wrong?"

"We believe that Mr. Brandon has taken some sensitive material from the bank, and we'd like to find it," said Smith.

"Before it gets him into more trouble," added Johnson.

Angela's eyes cut quickly to the envelope and the jump drive. Of course, Agent Smith caught the glance.

He picked up the jump drive. "Would this be from your ex-husband, Mrs. Harriman?"

She nodded. "Yes, that came in today's mail."

Agent Smith smiled. "Very good. May we keep it?"

Angela nodded. An annoyed look crossed her face. "Sure. I don't want anything from my ex-husband, believe me."

Agent Johnson had walked around behind her. "Is your husband home, Mrs. Harriman?"

She looked back at Johnson and shook her head. "Not yet. He will be home in about an hour."

"I see."

Agent Smith took a step closer to Angela. "And his name is...?"

Angela turned her attention back to Smith. "Allen."

Agent Johnson took a sand-filled sap from his pants pocket and hit Angela on the head with it. She slumped to the floor, unconscious.

ANGELA CAME TO GRADUALLY. Her head swam if she moved it very much, and it hurt like crazy. She was lying on her stomach, on the bed.

She opened her eyes. Her vision was very blurry, and it swam in and out of focus as she looked around.

The first thing she saw was her husband. Allen was tied to a wooden chair from the dinette set in the kitchen. His head was slumped down.

Angela tried to go to him, but she couldn't move her hands. Each hand was tied to one side of the bed's headboard. Each ankle was tied to one side of the footboard. She was spread-eagled on the bed, and she was naked.

A jolt of fear ran through her then.

"Allen!" she hissed. "Allen! Wake up!"

Allen jerked his head a bit, and groaned.

"Allen! Wake *up*, dammit!"

Her husband raised his head. "Wus wrong, baby?"

"Can you get loose?"

"Wha...?"

"Can you get loose from that chair?" Angela whispered.

From the door of the bedroom, a voice sounded. "If I had to guess, I'd say the answer is no."

The voice belonged to Agent Smith. Angela recognized it, and jumped in surprise...as much as the nylon ropes would allow, anyway.

"Please let us go. We'll keep quiet, no one will ever know," said Angela desperately.

"Could we please forego the 'begging for your life' part? It's so boring, and it won't help," replied Agent Smith.

Agent Johnson came into the bedroom. "Have you asked her yet?"

Agent Smith shot a quick glance at his partner. "No, not yet."

Agent Johnson came around to Angela's line of sight. "Mrs. Harriman, have you told anyone about the mail you received today from your ex-husband?"

Angela shook her head. "No, nobody."

"Did you maybe tell your husband here?"

"No, he hasn't even seen today's mail." Angela started crying. "*Why are you doing this to us?*"

Agent Johnson slapped Angela's exposed cheek. Hard. "*I'll ask the questions, bitch!*"

Allen chose that moment to fully wake up. "Hey! Who the hell are you, and what the hell are you doing?" His eyes were wide with astonishment and anger.

Agent Smith backhanded Allen. "Shut up." The chair rocked with the force of the backhand slap.

Angela burst into fresh tears, and screamed. Agent Johnson punched the side of Angela's head so hard that she almost passed out.

"Scream again, and I'll cut hubby's throat." Agent Johnson's tone was conversational. "Do you understand me?"

Angela didn't respond.

The rogue FBI agent grabbed a huge handful of Angela's hair and pulled hard. "I asked if you understand me."

Angela cried out, and then nodded.

Allen spoke up. "What are you going to do to us?"

Agent Smith smiled. "The man who pays us extra gave us instructions. He said that we were to find out who else knows about that mail from Mr. Brandon, and, once we find out what you both know, we are to kill you." His smile grew into a sadistic grin as he began wrapping grey duct tape around Allen's head, covering his mouth securely. "But he didn't say that we couldn't have fun before we kill you."

Agent Johnson smiled down at Angela. "We're going to take turns fucking you. When we're at the point that we can't get our dicks hard any more, we're going to slowly kill you." He took a strip of duct tape from another roll, and put it over Angela's mouth. "And we're going to let your dear hubby watch until you've drawn your last breath." He leaned close down to her ear. "Then we'll kill him, too."

AS AGENT SMITH SET fire to the gasoline he had poured inside the Harriman house, Agent Johnson tucked the brown bubble envelope that Michael Brandon had mailed to his ex-wife into his jacket pocket, along with the jump drive that had been inside.

Agent Smith walked out beside Agent Johnson. "We need to get several feet away before I set off the explosive in the bedroom."

Agent Johnson nodded. "I think the street should be far enough away. Did you use enough gasoline along with the explosive?"

Agent Smith looked at his partner. "Are you kidding? Of course I did. We've been doing his wet work for a while, remember."

The two FBI agents reached the street, and turned back to watch the house. They were waiting for the explosion.

They didn't have long to wait.

The explosives in the bedroom went off without a hitch. The gasoline in the room followed with a huge "*WHOOOMPF*", and the entire house was almost burned to the ground by the time firefighters arrived.

Hopefully, all evidence of the murders were burned away with the fire. Pieces of the explosive device would be found, and, as a matter of course, would be sent to the nearest FBI lab.

And the pieces would disappear.

When no evidence remained, no crime could be proven.

Agents Smith and Johnson's benefactor would be safe once more.

There remained one more matter to wrap up, and they would take care of that the next day.

With any luck, they'd be back to investigating non-existent terrorist threats in the heartland by tomorrow night.

JOSETTE LEBEAU WAS the Postmaster (or postmistress, depending on your point of view) of the Tucker's Corner branch of the United States Post Office. She often worked the window alone, and performed the sorting of the P. O. Box mail at the same time.

Josette was proud of her work, and of her memory. Package delivery services often stopped in to her small post office to ask where they could find particular addresses. Josette was able to provide not only directions, but often where the person could be found if they weren't at home.

She loved living in a small town. It made things so simple.

Some people liked to say that Josette often had her nose in business that wasn't hers. But, that wasn't quite the case. Being a Postmaster meant handling a lot of mail, and she couldn't be blamed for recognizing return addresses. It was her job, after all. If prodded, Josette could tell you who was being hounded by collection agencies, who was receiving paper pension checks, who invested in the stock market, and who was buying and selling a lot online. Many of the other things were now being done online as well, like investment services and direct deposit, but not all...and Josette could tell you all of them.

If she wanted to.

But, Josette wasn't the kind of person to broadcast what she knew. She played her knowledge like a poker hand...close to her chest. Sometimes, she quietly showed up at someone's house that seemed to be in financial trouble, bringing in a load of groceries. Or, sometimes, she would see that enough cash was left to pay a delinquent electric or water bill. She was rarely caught doing what she did with those payments, but she couldn't hide the grocery deliveries.

Josette came from a very poor family, led by a drunken, overbearing father that, when drunk, was a little too free with his fists. Often, what little money

her father had been able to make was immediately spent at a local tavern.
When he came home drunk, penniless, and angry, he took his frustration out
on his family. Josette's mother had borne the brunt of the brutal attacks, but
she and her brother had also had their share of beatings, too. One day, when
he was seventeen, Josette's brother had enough, and had beaten their father
into a coma. Her father never woke up, and the decision was made to pull the
plug. No tears were shed, and the family fabricated a story that the man was
beaten by someone in the alley behind the tavern. Josette's mother now lived
a comfortable life in California, and her brother worked in Silicon Valley, and
supported their mother easily.

Josette had stayed behind, and took the test for the United States Postal
Service. She had passed the test easily, and had climbed up the ladder until she
earned this Postmaster job.

Josette was thirty years old, and single. She had been seeing a gentleman
that worked at the insurance agency in town, and had begun to feel that the
relationship was going somewhere.

Josette was happy.

That morning, she was alone in the building that morning, as usual. Josette
was sorting mail into the boxes. The talk of the town that morning from her
customers had been all about the disappearance of Michael Brandon, and the
deaths of his ex-wife and her new husband. Many of the people that came in had
decided that Brandon had something to do with their deaths, and the police
chief had confirmed that some pieces of a timer and traces of explosive had been
found in the bedroom. Personally, Josette didn't know what to think, and was
just starting to digest the news, when the bell on the front door rang.

"Be right with you!" she called, and finished putting out the mail she held.
She walked around the divider to find two men in off-the-rack business suits.

"Good morning!" Josette said cheerfully. "May I help you gentlemen?"

The taller of the two opened a small leather wallet, displaying an FBI ID
card and a Federal badge.

"I'm Agent Johnson, ma'am, and this is my partner, Agent Smith."

Josette was impressed, but didn't show it. "And what can I do for the FBI
this morning?"

Agent Smith had hung back, staying near the front door.

Agent Johnson took out the small, brown, padded envelope that he had taken from Angela Harriman's home. He held it out for Josette to see.

"Do you remember the man that mailed this?"

Josette started to shake her head, then remembered who had mailed it. "Michael Brandon."

"And you see that it's addressed to Angela Harriman? His ex-wife?"

Josette nodded. "Of course I do."

"Was there anything unusual about the transaction?"

Josette thought about it for a moment, and then shook her head. "No. Nothing unusual, really."

"Are you certain?"

The Postmaster shook her head again. "No, nothing. All three were addressed properly, and he bought the proper postage for each one." *Wow, the FBI is looking into Michael's disappearance! Must be something big,* she thought to herself.

Agent Johnson's eyes had widened in surprise. "Did you say 'all three', Ms..." he glanced at her name tag, "...LeBeau?"

Josette nodded. "Yes, he mailed three envelopes."

"Can you remember who they were addressed to?"

Agent Smith had quietly reached over and flipped the lock on the front door. He flipped the simple sign hanging on the door so that it said "Closed".

Josette didn't notice. She was thinking hard, trying to remember who the addressees had been. "Let's see...there was this one, to Angie..."

Agent Johnson was encouraging. "Yes? Go on."

Josette laughed. "One was addressed to himself. The address looked like some mail drop over in Nevada. Reno, I think it was."

"Do you remember the address?"

Josette thought hard. "No, I'm sorry. I don't."

The FBI agent was excited. "And the third one?"

Josette truly was having trouble remembering. "It was a security company, in a city."

"Which city?"

Josette told him.

"And the name of the security company?"

Josette was shaking her head. "I'm sorry, Agent. I simply don't remember. It did have an odd name, though...I remember that. And it had a man's name, and it was in care of the security company...but I just can't remember the names. I'm sorry."

Agent Johnson's mouth settled into a grim line. "So am I, Ms. LeBeau." He reached out quickly, grabbed the back of Josette's head, and slammed it onto the counter, scattering stamp displays and postal forms everywhere.

Agent Smith climbed over the counter, and took Josette behind the divider. He slammed her down into a rolling swivel chair, and handcuffed her to it with two pairs of handcuffs.

"My *dose!*" said Josette wonderingly. She was dazed from the impact. "Daddy, why did you break my *dose?*"

Agent Johnson had joined Agent Smith, and now leaned down into Josette's face. "Sorry about your nose." He pulled out a disposable lighter, and flicked the flame to life. "But, we have to make sure that you don't remember who that package was addressed to...then we'll take you to see Michael Brandon."

Josette screamed, and begged for the pain to stop, but she simply could not remember the name on the envelope.

THE TWO MEN CLAIMING to be FBI agents did indeed take Josette to see Michael Brandon, although her hands were firmly cuffed, and her feet were weighted down with cement blocks. When Michael's waterlogged face had turned toward her, Josette screamed...and then, only drew in water from the city's reservoir.

Chapter 2

E mily Owens thoroughly enjoyed her job.

Emily was one of those secretaries that had progressed to the executive level, and she had done it through skill and hard work. She was very proud of the position that she occupied, and of the company that employed her.

Emily was not only the executive secretary, she was also occasionally in charge. She was not a vain woman. Far from it. But, when the call came, it came from necessity, so she stepped right up and took control. She usually made the correct decisions, and received praise from both her employer and her co-workers.

Right now, however, Emily was making coffee in her boss's private office. He liked a dark roast, and he liked it strong, and she was glad to comply.

Emily had, throughout her multi-year career, had other employment offers, but she had never accepted them. They might have offered more money than what she was taking home right now, but many employers didn't realize that money, while important, wasn't everything in a job. Often, a job provided satisfaction, variety, and a sense of accomplishment. Emily didn't want to give those things up.

She turned, and looked again at the inner sanctum of her employer's workplace. It had two huge floor-to-ceiling, arched, Gothic-style windows. One window faced east, and the other faced south. For most of the day, bright sunlight shone poured into the office. The office itself was on the top floor of the Sullivan building downtown, a few blocks over from Hooker Hollow, along with all of the other office buildings.

She sat down at her desk, and began sifting through overnight reports. Emily had to have them in coherent order for her employer, because he liked to be able to get an impression from them at first glance, then, later, go through them in detail.

The receptionist, Lena Marrucci, knocked quietly as she entered the private office.

"Good morning, Miss Owens."

Emily smiled. "Good morning, Lena."

Lena had an armful of paper and packages. "The mail's here." She put it all on a corner of Emily's desk.

"Anything interesting in it, Lena?"

Lena shook her head. "I don't know, ma'am. I have people in the outer office, and I didn't take the time to go through it."

Emily chuckled. Unless the office were on fire, Lean *always* 'had people'. "Just remember, those 'people' pay our salaries, Lena."

Lena smiled shyly. "Yes, ma'am, I know." She started to leave, then turned back. "His nine-thirty is here early."

Emily nodded. "I'll tell him when he gets here. Thank you."

"Yes, ma'am." Lena turned and left the office.

Emily smiled a smug little smile to herself. *Girl's never going to be more than a receptionist here. Unless the boss takes a personal interest in her, and tries to teach her a few things.*

Emily told herself to stop thinking snarky thoughts.

She glanced at the pile of mail as she sorted through the overnight reports. A couple of packages, three or four padded envelopes, and a lot of what looked like checks. Good. At least they'd make payroll this week. They'd never missed one yet, but, sometimes, it was a close thing.

Emily had just finished getting the reports in order when she heard the *snick* of the office's private entrance. She looked up at her employer with a smile on her face. *Nine o'clock on the nose. Every morning. You can set your watch by him.*

"Good morning, boss," said Emily, with a smile. She stood behind her desk. "I have the morning reports all ready for you."

Her employer smiled back, his white, shiny teeth twinkling in the morning light from the window. "I can always count on you, Emily." He walked over to her desk and took the reports.

Oh, dear God, his resemblance to a young Tom Selleck is astounding! Emily's heart beat with a distant, never-going-to-happen lust for her employer. "The coffee will be ready in just a few minutes, sir."

Already skimming the overnight reports, her boss responded with a distracted tone. "Thank you, Emily." He walked over to his own desk, a big walnut-colored wood thing, with multiple drawers, and a couple of hidden drawers, too. He had told her that it had descended from the writer Rex Stout, and that he had used it to write the first Nero Wolfe novel back in the nineteen-thirties. He told her that he had papers to prove it, but she had never seen them.

As her employer settled in behind his desk, deep into scanning the reports, Emily's desk phone rang. She picked it up.

"Jim Dandy Security, this is Emily. How may I help you?"

The voice on the other end was low and throaty. "You can tell me what you're wearin', baby...then tell me when you gonna take it off."

"Excuse me?"

"I didn't stutter, baby...tell me what you wearin'."

Emily smiled. "What's going on, honey? Are you bored during their meeting again?"

"Dang, woman, you s'posed to play along!"

With mock playfulness, Emily said, "Oh, I'm sorry, honey. I'm wearing a leather teddy...crotchless...with long, shiny hip boots. And I have a whip."

"Hmph. Don't play so rough, babe."

Emily laughed. "See you tonight?"

"Yeah, baby. Unless somethin' comes up."

"Oh, something will come up tonight. Count on it."

The voice on the other end laughed and hung up.

"Does Joey Justice know that his executive secretary is seeing another executive secretary? And she's one that works for his competition?" Jim was smirking as he spoke.

Emily tossed her hair. "Turk is a good man. Like you. And so is Joey Justice. He wouldn't say a word if he knew."

Jim nodded. "Ah. So he doesn't know."

Emily looked sheepish, then smirked. "No. He doesn't. But Turk and I don't talk about work at all."

Jim smiled again, and his teeth sparkled once more. "I know that, Emmy. I've heard your side of the nine o'clock conversations for several weeks now." He had completed the skimming portion of the reports, and now he was about to read through them. "Good thing they have that meeting every morning at nine, isn't it?"

Emily turned toward her boss. "Jim, you don't really mind that I'm seeing Turk Wendell, do you?"

Jim answered with a distracted tone. "Of course not, Em. I would have said something by now if I did."

"Thank you." Emily turned back to her desk, and began sorting the mail. When she had finished, she picked up the things that she thought might be important, and put them on Jim's desk.

Jim looked up at Emily. "Anything interesting?"

She pointed at the pile. "I think you got something from that friend of yours in Oregon. It's postmarked Tucker's Corner."

Jim smiled. Twinkle. "Great! I need to call him. I haven't spoken to him for almost six months."

"Would you like me to place the call?"

Jim shook his head. "No, it's too early there right now. Let's wait until later in the day, and I'll get in touch with him then."

"Yes, sir." Emily returned to her desk and began working. Abruptly, she turned again. "Oh, I forgot to tell you – your nine-thirty is here already."

"And his appointment is...?"

"Nine-thirty."

"So I'll see him at...?"

"Nine-thirty."

"Correct."

"Yes, sir." Emily returned to work.

At nine twenty-eight, Jim said, "You can tell Lena to send in Mr. Abbott now, Em. I'm sorry if I seemed abrupt. One of those reports disturbed me. I think Zuckerman is lying. I think he's been sleeping all through his shift."

"Do you want me to set up an appointment with him, Jim?"

Jim Dandy shook his head. "No, thank you. I believe I'll just drop in on him tonight...and make sure that he's doing the job properly."

Emily smiled as she picked up the phone. "Yes, sir. Lena, please send Mr. Abbott in now." She stood to greet the client.

AFTER LUNCH, JIM FOUND a moment to open his mail. The first to be opened were the ones that resembled checks. Most were, indeed, checks, and he assembled them, endorsed them, and gave them to Emily for deposit.

He began opening packages once the checks had been done. The first package was full of 8x10 photos of a philandering husband and his mistress inside a motel room on the outskirts of the city. They had left the windows open, and Jim's operative had gotten some excellent digital shots, and had them blown up to 8x10s. Jim set them aside to show to the suspicious wife later. Another fee in the bag, more if they had to testify in court. Usually, in divorce cases nowadays, the only time Jim's people had to testify was if one spouse wanted more than half the property...but the photos made good evidence for their clients.

The second package contained a sample. Sellers of security merchandise often sent samples of their products to Jim Dandy Security in the hope of selling enough to supply each of his uniformed people. This time, they had sent an extendable metal baton, five inches long, that expanded out to just over two feet when you flicked it. Jim played with it a few minutes, until it jammed and wouldn't go back to its storage length. *Sample didn't last five minutes. Piece of junk.* He tossed the baton and the package that contained it into his trash can. *Can't let one of my people trust their lives, or someone else's life, to a piece of junk that breaks in five minutes.*

The third package was the one with the Tucker's Corner postmark. Jim smiled to himself and opened the small, padded envelope. He peeked inside, and took out a jump drive and a piece of paper. The piece of paper was a hastily written note that said:

Dear Jim,

I'm sorry to dump this on you, but I don't know anyone else that can deal with it. This jump drive contains information that I found by accident, and I'm afraid it has marked me for death.

In it, you'll find deposits made to some mystery person. They came from an offshore account used by the Mexican drug cartel leader, Esteban Fernandez. They're rather large sums of money, and they're being systematically deposited into another offshore account, but I won't be able to find out who owns that account before they kill me.

When I spotted this information, I immediately made three copies. One I mailed to myself, at a mail drop in Reno. Another went to Angela. You have the third. An hour after I made the copies, the data disappeared, and my regional manager called me on the phone. From his remarks, I know that he knew about the payments, and he knew that I had copied the files. I also knew that I would not be long for this world because of it.

Be careful with looking into this, and don't get yourself killed!

I'll always be your friend. Thanks.

Michael

Jim's brow furrowed as he read the letter a second time. He then held up the jump drive and looked at it, lost in thought.

He turned to his computer and found the phone number for the Tucker's Corner branch of Second Fidelity Bank. Picking up his landline phone, he dialed the necessary digits to set up an untraceable call, then dialed the bank's number. A woman on the other end answered.

"Second Fidelity Bank. How may I direct your call?"

Jim adopted a deep Southern drawl. "Hi. Ah'd like to talk to Michael Brandon, please."

There was a pause on the other end. "I'm sorry, sir, but Mr. Brandon no longer works here."

Jim gave a fake laugh. "Aw, come on! He's been there forevah! What, is he hidin' in the bathroom?"

Another pause. "No, sir, he really doesn't work here anymore. He's disappeared."

"Disappeahed?"

"Yes, sir, I'm sorry. Could I direct your call to Mr. Utley? He's our regional manager. Perhaps he could help you."

Jim was definitely feeling something off about this conversation. The pauses that the woman made fueled that feeling. "No, thank ya, ma'am, I'll just give his ex-wife a call. He owes her money, so she always knows where he is."

Another slight pause. "You don't know?"

Jim's instincts were really tingling now. "Know what, ma'am?"

"Mr. Brandon's ex-wife was killed. So was her husband. Their house exploded, and burned to the ground. With Mr. Brandon's disappearance...well...you know." Another slight pause. "What did you say your name was, sir?"

Jim casually put the phone down on the receiver, and leaned back in his chair. His mind was whirling with the implications of the phone call. Michael was gone, his ex-wife was dead...he abruptly turned again to his computer, and typed words into his search engine, looking for local news for that county in Oregon.

The first two hits were bland stories. One was about a Tucker's Corner city council meeting that had almost erupted into a fistfight. The second story concerned the explosion at Angie Harriman's home.

Jim read that one all the way through.

The third story concerned the disappearance of the Tucker's Corner Postmaster, Josette LaBeau. She had apparently just locked the front door and walked away from the Post Office, but had left her vehicle. The story asked anyone with any information to call police.

Postmaster...and Michael... and Angie. All dead. All about the same time. So, why would a Postmaster disappear around the same time?

His eyes fell on Michael's scribbled note. He re-read the part that said, "*One I mailed to myself, at a mail drop in Reno. Another went to Angela. You have the third.*"

The answer hit him so quickly that his heart jumped. He turned quickly to look at the padded envelope again, with its big, round Tucker's Corner postmark.

Oh, shit! he thought to himself.

Jim turned again to his computer, and, in his search engine, typed in "News Reno Mail Drop".

The first hit was a news story from the Reno newspaper, dated two days earlier. It told about a mail and package service that had been destroyed by a fire and an explosion. The clerk was killed in the fire, and there was suspicion of arson. Fire experts were investigating.

Jim Dandy had to assume that whoever had done all of that knew about the third jump drive.

And where Michael had mailed it.

And its final destination.

Jim picked up the jump drive and envelope, and exited through his private office entrance.

Chapter 3

O utside, Jim ducked into the alley beside the Sullivan building, and carefully burned the envelope. Once it was ash, he walked to the parking garage in the basement of the building, got into his new Corvette Convertible, and drove to the main branch of the city's public library.

I miss my Chrysler Sebring Convertible. I always thought it was a sharp car.

Once inside the library, Jim asked for access to a computer. He specifically asked for one without Internet access, and got it. He sat down, turned on the machine, and inserted the jump drive.

On the screen, the files on the jump drive auto-started, and displayed a spreadsheet. The spreadsheet contained two pages of listings that documented several payments of several thousand dollars each. The account that the money came from was shown, and Jim assumed that it was the one that Michael had written that was used by Esteban Fernandez. The other account, signified only by a group of numbers, was a mystery. Both banks were in the Cayman Islands, and were well-known to be simply stopping points for money passing through, as it made its way to other locations. The money then went through Second Fidelity, and into a numbered account somewhere else. All of this information, convoluted as it was, proved the old adage of "follow the money" was a true saying.

Jim studied the spreadsheet. Whoever was receiving the payments was getting a lot of money from Fernandez. But who? And why?

He selected "print" from the spreadsheet menu, and printed five copies. As he sat at the library computer, he noticed that the light for the Internet had gone from red to green. Jim sat back and looked at the light for a moment, and realized that he had to have triggered something on the jump drive that automatically sent a message over the Internet, since he had specifically asked for no Internet connection. Apparently, he had been misunderstood, and the Internet had only been turned off instead of disconnected.

The light went from green back to red. The entire Internet message had taken less than thirty seconds. If he hadn't been sitting in front of the computer, he never would have noticed.

Jim quickly made a decision. He pulled out the jump drive, gathered his materials, and quickly left the library.

Thank God I didn't use my real name!

He climbed into the Corvette, started it up, and began driving back to the office. He noticed a generic four-door sedan that stopped in front of the library, but he didn't hang around to see who had been in it.

The security man inside him began thinking. *Who has that kind of technology? And who can respond that quickly?* He didn't know, but it was time to take out some insurance.

And time to hide a few key pieces of evidence.

Jim Dandy drove to the downtown YMCA. Using one of his aliases, he rented a room and a storage locker, and paid a month's rent for both. Inside the locker, he placed the jump drive and the printed pages he had made. He reached inside his coat pocket to get the letter that Michael had written so that he could hide it with the other material, but it wasn't inside his coat. He smacked his forehead as he remembered that he had left the letter on his desk. *Crap!*

He closed the locker, and put on a padlock in addition to the combination lock the locker already had. He walked back to his car, got in, and drove back to the office.

Jim entered the office through his private entrance, and Emily was waiting.

"Emmy." Jim's voice was upbeat, but Emily could sense something was wrong.

Michael's letter was on Jim's desk, in plain sight.

Emily looked up from her work. "Yes, sir?"

Jim picked up the letter. "Did you read this?"

Emily nodded. "Was that okay?"

Jim folded the letter, and hid it in his sock. He turned to her. "That's fine, Emily, but you never read it. You never saw it, and you don't know what mail came today. As a matter of fact, I believe you feel ill, and might need to get out of town for a while."

"No, sir." Emily wasn't an idiot. She knew when her boss was in trouble, and could usually guess what caused it. It had to be that letter. "What was on the jump drive?"

Jim looked stern. "Emily..."

"No, *sir.*" She adopted her own stern look. "I haven't avoided trouble since I started working for you, and I don't plan to start now."

"Emily, this could be dangerous. You could get killed, if what I *think* is happening *is* happening."

"And I could be killed by a burglar in my apartment, or a mugger on the street. You can't do it alone, Jim. I won't let you." She crossed her arms defiantly. "Now what was on the jump drive?"

Jim shook his head with a silly grin on his face. "Okay, Emily, but no further than this office."

"It never is."

Jim explained what the letter said, the news he had found on the Internet, what he had discovered on the jump drive, what had happened at the library, and what he had done with the evidence.

"Wow." Emily frowned. "Jim, this is big. Well, anything connected with Esteban Fernandez is big, anyway, but *this*...what should we do?"

"Well, right now, one of us needs to go to the Y and put this letter in with the rest of the evidence."

"Do you want me to do it?"

"Do you mind, Emmy?"

Emily smiled. "Not at all, Jim." She stood, preparing to leave, when the phone on her desk rang. It was the office intercom. Emily answered it. "Emily Owens."

"This is Lena. There are two men from the government out here to see Mr. Dandy."

"Okay, Lena, just a minute." She put the call on hold, and turned to Jim. "Lena is on hold. She says that two men from the government are outside, waiting to see you."

"Appointment?"

"No, sir."

"Okay. Go ahead and take the letter to the Y...here's the key for the padlock, and I've written down the combination for you." He handed the key and the sticky note to Emily. She tucked them into her purse, along with the letter. "Leave by the private entrance."

"Yes, sir." Emily left.

Jim picked up his desk phone, and pressed the intercom button. "Lena, you can send them in now, please."

"Yes, sir, Mr. Dandy."

Jim's office door opened, and two men in off-the-rack black business suits entered.

Jim stood and walked over to meet the two men. "Hello. I'm Jim Dandy." He held out his hand.

The first man shook it. "Mr. Dandy. I'm Hugh Mitchell, and this is Randy Norfleet. We're from the Internal Revenue Service."

Jim had a talent – his face seldom reflected what he was feeling inside. Inside, he was panicking, because he didn't know why the IRS would be here, and he hoped that the damned accountants hadn't screwed something up. Outside, the smile never left his face, and the twinkle remained.

"Come in, gentlemen. Please sit down, and tell me what Jim Dandy Security can do for the IRS."

The two men sat across from Jim. Mitchell opened his briefcase, and said, "Mr. Dandy, we're here because the IRS is auditing taxes for the past five years of all security firms in the city."

"I see. And I suppose you have proper paperwork authorizing that function, and proper identification?"

Mitchell smiled, and produced a letter. It was printed on official IRS letterhead, and did indeed authorize what Mitchell had stated. When Jim finished reading the letter, he looked up, and both men had their IDs out for Jim to examine.

Satisfied that they were the real deal, Jim asked a question. "Okay, gentlemen, what do you need from me?"

"All paperwork and tax forms from the last five years, an office to work in, and, if they're available, your accountants."

Jim opened his hands. "Not a problem, Mr. Mitchell." He picked up his desk phone, and asked Lena to come in.

When Lena entered the office, Jim gave her instructions. "Lena, please show these two gentlemen from the IRS to an empty office, and get them whatever they need. And please ask the people from our accounting firm to join them."

Lena glanced at the two IRS agents, then back at Jim. "Yes, sir." To the visitors, she said, "Would you follow me, please?"

The men stood, and so did Jim.

Jim told them, "If you need anything from me, please let me know."

Norfleet nodded his acknowledgement. "We will, Mr. Dandy."

Mitchell said, "Thank you."

Once the office door closed behind the two men, Jim collapsed into his chair, letting his arms hang down the sides. *Great. What else can happen?*

His cell phone rang. Jim hung his head, and then he pulled it out. Emily.

He answered. "What's wrong, Emily?"

"The man at the desk won't let me back to the lockers. He says the 'M' in YMCA says it all."

Shaking his head in disbelief, Jim replied. "On my way, Emmy. Sit tight."

"Yes, sir."

They hung up.

Jim looked around the office for a moment. He picked up his desk phone and dialed Lena.

"Lena, I have to go out for a while. Emily is out, too. You're in charge."

"Yes, sir."

Jim exited the office through the private entrance again. On his way to the Y, he thought about the situation with Michael's information. *Should I give it to the IRS, or should I just wait to see what happens? I'm leaning toward waiting, just to see if I can get some nibbles on this bait.*

The first thing on my list? I need to find out what that jump drive triggered. And I think I know who can help me with that one.

Chapter 4

"I said, we're here to see Joey Justice," said one of the two men in off-the-rack business suits.

"And I said that you aren't going anywhere until I find out if he's seeing visitors," replied Tony Armstrong from behind the reception desk in the Justice Security building.

Justice Security, Incorporated owned its own building on a tree-lined street in a better part of the city. The six-story aboveground edifice occupied a large portion of a city block, with parking areas for visitors, and a landscaped, park-like green area on its south side. The building itself was constructed of three-foot-wide reinforced concrete walls. Each window was made of thick bulletproof glass, including the visitors' entrance door. The building extended six floors underground. The bottom three underground floors were used as a vehicle storage area, and housed various armor-plated and bullet resistant vehicles to be used as protective equipment for transporting and defending employees or clients. The next underground level was the armory. All types of weapons were stored in the climate-controlled armory, from revolvers and automatic pistols, to mortars, to surface-to-air missiles and launchers, and various armor-piercing weapons. Enough weaponry and ammunition were stored in the armory to take down a small country's government, should they be hired for such a thing...and they had done so, twice, a couple of years ago under an ultra-classified government contract. The floor above the armory was records storage. This floor contained the paper files, computers, data storage, and research areas needed for executing and completing client contracts. The final underground level was the garage for employee parking, and was accessed by a ground-level entrance contained by a thick, heavy steel door embedded into the concrete walls of the building.

At ground level, the first floor contained the reception area, the cafeteria, building security, the medical facility, and visitors' lounge. The second and third floors were occupied by employee offices, conference rooms, smaller meeting rooms, and clerical services, along with the employee gym. The fourth floor housed executive offices and the situation room. The fifth floor was for guest housing, and the top floor contained residential apartments for the top level people of the company. The roof of the building had a helicopter pad, equipped with two armor-reinforced, stealth-equipped, black ops helicopters always ready to fly at a moment's notice. The company also owned two private jets and two large cargo planes, which were housed at a private airfield just south of the city.

Justice Security had been formed a few years earlier by four college friends, who remained the directors and sole stockholders of the company.

Joey Justice, after whom the company was named, was a nondescript man. Standing at five feet ten inches, he had dark hair and intense brown eyes that usually missed nothing. He had founded the company with the premise of providing security services tempered with justice, as his name implied. He was very much in love with the lady in his life, who was also one of the cofounders of the company.

Misty Wilhite, the lady of Joey's life, stood five feet five. She had shoulder-length auburn hair, with green eyes. She was extremely attractive, but she had a punch that could drop a person twice her size. She, too, was very much in love with Joey, and shared his belief of security and justice. They had not married yet, but had just become engaged.

Dexter Beck was the resident computer nerd. Standing one inch taller than Misty, Dexter was consistently underestimated by antagonists. Understanding usually followed, because Dexter also was a martial arts master, utilizing several methods of self-defense. The security and computer systems used by Justice Security were created, programmed, and maintained by Dexter.

Percival "King Louie" Washington was the fourth founding member of Justice Security. Louie stood four inches over six feet, and had a very imposing muscular build. He also was very intelligent and street-smart. His skin was the color of a chocolate bar, and he kept his head shaved. The other three founding members had nicknamed him "King Louie" in their first year of college because of his unfortunate facial resemblance to the cartoon character in the Jungle Book movie. It wasn't racial, and Louie knew it...just like if he had had a big nose, they would have nicknamed him "Baloo". Besides, anything was better than his given name of Percy.

Recent additions to the partners included Jessica Queen, the former executive secretary to the four partners. Her immediate replacement, Patti Hoehn, had been tortured, killed and mutilated by Esteban Fernandez, who had caught her on the street snapping photos during the company's first encounter with him. Patti's replacement, Turk Wendell, was a huge, hulking man, who was surprisingly adept at performing secretarial duties.

Another addition to the partners had been Dexter Beck's right hand person, Megan Fisk Beck. She had led an attempted pre-emptive attack on Fernandez, and had gotten wounded in the process. She and Dexter had eloped, and were happily married newlyweds.

"I told you that we're from the government!"

"I don't care if you're Rapid Roy the Stock Car Boy! You're not getting inside this building without the boss's approval!" Tony glared at the two men. "Unless you have a warrant, I would suggest you sit down and behave yourselves, and I'll call up to see if the boss has time to see you."

The two men glared at Tony, and Tony glared back, with his right hand resting on his belt. Above his holster. Daring the two men to defy him.

The men chose not to defy Tony. They sat down in the visitors' area, and steamed.

"Thank you, gentlemen." Tony picked up the phone to call upstairs.

Tony was in charge of the uniformed security officers at Justice Security. The uniformed officers were nicknamed 'grunts' within the company. Tony also ran the front desk, and dealt with visitors to the building...sometimes forcefully, if necessary.

Turk Wendell answered the phone. "Turk."

"Hey, Turk." Tony was still glowering at the two men. "I got two government men down here. They want to see Joey."

"He free right now. Lemme see does he wanna talk to 'em. Call you back."

"I'll be here." Tony hung up.

"They're checking with Mr. Justice. They'll call me back." He openly stared at the two men, daring them to say something.

The two men sat quietly, neither one caring to say anything that might anger Tony enough to throw them out of the building.

Tony's phone rang. "Front desk, Tony."

"Joey say send 'em up." Turk was blunt with his friend.

Tony was just as blunt. "I'll bring them up in just a minute." He hung up, and took out his radio. When he pressed the transmit key, he said, "King. Ferguson. Come to the front desk please. Now."

Tony had barely put his radio back on his belt when Brandon King and Patty Ferguson came out of the cafeteria and down the walkway to the reception desk.

"What's wrong, Tony?" Patty looked concerned.

Tony looked at the two young grunts. "Nothing. I want you two to babysit the front desk while I escort those two gentlemen to the fourth floor."

Both young people glanced at the two men, then came around behind the desk.

Tony got very close to them, and talked to them in a very low voice. "There's something about these two that I don't like. They tried to bull their way in here. When I leave with them, I want you to call Turk, tell him what I just told you, and ask him to pass it along to Joey."

"Yes, sir," replied Brandon.

Tony nodded at the two of them, then went around and stood in front of the men from the government. "Mr. Justice will see you. I'm to escort you there. Follow me, please."

The two men rose, and followed Tony to the elevators.

Back at the front desk, Patty was hanging up the phone after informing Turk. "I wonder who those guys were?"

Brandon shrugged. "I don't know, but they pissed Tony off pretty bad. He usually doesn't let something like that show."

Patty smiled. "Maybe they're from the IRS. Tony doesn't like the IRS at all."

Brandon looked at her with incredulity. "And just how the hell do you know *that?*"

Patty wore a prim smile as she said, "I guess you'll just have to wonder, won't you?"

"HELLO, MR. JUSTICE. I'm Jim Gilbert, and this is Harold Purvis. We're from the IRS."

Joey nodded his greeting to the two men, and gestured to the two chairs facing his desk. "Hello, gentlemen. Please sit down."

Tony was standing at Joey's office door. "You okay, sir?"

Joey, knowing how badly Tony disliked the IRS, smiled. "We're fine, Tony, thank you."

Tony nodded at Joey. He turned and left the room, and closed the door behind him.

Joey spoke to his guests. "Gentlemen, please excuse Tony's behavior. He...well, he doesn't care very much for the IRS."

Gilbert frowned. "Very few people do, Mr. Justice."

Joey nodded. "So, what can I do for the IRS today, gentlemen?"

Gilbert opened his briefcase and took out a couple of papers. He reached across to place the papers on the desk. "Mr. Justice, for some reason, orders came down from Washington, instructing our office here in the city to audit every security firm's taxes for the last five years. I have no idea why, but we have to do it."

Joey nodded. "I understand. I'm guessing that you need our accountants, correct?"

Purvis replied, "Yes, if you don't mind."

"You'll find that they're the best in the business. We actually have a couple of former IRS accountants working for us." Joey stood, and walked around the desk. "If you gentlemen will come with me, I'll take you to our Accounting department. They're on the second floor."

The men rose, with their arms laden with briefcases, and prepared to follow Joey.

Joey stopped at the office door. "Just one thing, gentlemen. May I please see your IDs?"

The men looked at Joey.

Joey blandly looked back. He had deliberately waited until they had risen and picked up all of their paraphernalia before asking for ID, and they knew he had done it on purpose.

But, once asked, they were required to show their ID.

The men set everything down on the two armchairs in Joey's office, dug out their wallets with ID cards, and displayed them to Joey.

Joey looked closely at the ID cards, and was satisfied that they were genuine.

"Thank you, gentlemen. Please follow me."

Joey led the way out of the office. He was smiling to himself.

MCFEELY'S BAR WAS ON Third Street downtown. Third Street had another name that reflected most of the business conducted there.

Third Street was also Hooker Hollow.

McFeely's was known on the streets as "McFeelme's". It was known for serving hard drinks to hard people. Many criminal elements patronized Hank McFeely's establishment, but the rules were straightforward. If you're doing something illegal, you took it outside. If you started a fight, Hank finished it. If you were looking for someone, Hank might help you find them...if he liked you.

Jim Dandy and Emily Owens entered McFeely's after six o'clock. Jim was looking for a man that could often be found spending time in McFeely's. Jim was hoping that that man was there tonight.

Jim's sport coat was blue, and he wore a maroon shirt with jeans. Emily still wore her work suit, with the dark gray herringbone patterned skirt, white shirt, and gray jacket. They looked like people that had just left work, and wanted a drink before going home. Of course, Hank knew who Jim was, so the outfit only fooled some of the less-than-stellar clientele.

Jim and Emily both sat at the bar. Michelle, Hank's bartender, waved a small finger wave at Jim. Michelle had blonde hair, round wire glasses, a few freckles across her nose, and a smile that most men would love to have turned their way. Jim had helped Michelle with a small stalker problem once, at no charge, and Michelle had been grateful to him ever since. Hank liked Jim, too, although he thought that Jim was a little too fancy for McFeely's.

"Hi, Hank! Hi, Michelle! Busy tonight?" asked Jim.

Hank shrugged. "Meh. So-so, I guess. What's up, Jim?"

"I'm looking for a guy tonight, Hank...maybe you can help me."

"I will if I can. As long as nothing happens inside."

Jim shook his head, and flashed his hundred-watt smile. "Nothing like that, Hank. I just need some information...maybe some computer help."

Hank nodded his understanding. "You need Snickers, don't you?"

Jim raised his eyebrows. "Is he here, Hank?"

Hank smirked. "Yeah, he's here. Last booth on the left."

"Thanks, Hank. You're great!"

Hank waved Jim off. "Yeah, yeah. Good to see you again, Jim. You too, Emily."

Emily smiled demurely. "Thank you, Hank. Hello, Michelle."

Michelle smiled at Emily. "Hi, Emily. Nice to see you."

Jim stood. "Would you ask Hazel to bring us each a drink, Hank? I'll take rum and diet cola. What would you like, Emily?"

"A glass of white wine, please." She stood. "The good stuff, too, Hank."

"Whatever you'd like, Emily." Hank went to work making their drinks.

Jim led the way down the aisle between the private booths. He held Emily's hand as he led her along the aisle. He nodded at acquaintances along the way. At one point, he whispered into Emily's ear. "Lot of bad guys here tonight, Emmy. Stay alert."

Emily nodded her understanding.

Finally, they reached the end of the aisle. A small, ratty little man sat in the booth on the left, nursing a beer. Another man sat in the booth with him. They obviously had been talking, because the second man abruptly said, "See ya, Snick" and got out of the booth.

Snickers, the only name that Jim knew the man by, looked up at the security man. "Well, you know, you could have, you know, called or something. I would have made sure that, you know, I was alone when you, you know, got here."

Jim smiled and held out his hand. Snickers took it, and the men shook.

Word on the street was that Snickers had been a junkie, busted by Nicholas Turner wayyy back when Turner was still a cop. Snickers had offered information and a promise to get clean in exchange for making the charges go away. Nicholas had taken Snickers at his work, and the information had checked out. Word was that Nicholas paid for rehab for Snickers, and that he had been clean ever since. He had a knack for computers, and made his living with them. He still had the nervous twitches and still had the nervous speech pattern that he had developed as a junkie.

"Hi, Snickers," said Jim. "It's nice to see you again." He indicated Emily. "This is my executive secretary, Emily."

Snickers smiled at Emily. "Hi, Emily. Wow. Looks like Jim's, you know, comin' up in the world." He gestured to the booth seat that the other man had just vacated. "Why don't you two, you know, sit down?"

Emily sat down and slid across the seat. Jim joined her.

"So, you know, what can I do for you?"

Jim smiled his hundred-watt-smile. "Snickers!"

Snickers looked at Emily as he held a hand out indicating Jim. "Can you, you know, believe this guy? The only time, you know, that I see that big shit-eating, modeling grin on him, you know, is when he wants something on the, you know, cheap!"

Emily smiled at Snickers demurely.

Snickers couldn't look away. "Wow. Now, *that* smile, you know, I'd move the world for. Wow." Snickers shook his head as if to clear it. "Wow," he said again. He looked at Jim. "Awright, ya dime-store Tom Selleck, you know, wannabe. What do you, you know, need from me today?"

"I need your computer skills, Snickers." Jim held up the jump drive. "This has something on it, and I don't know what it is, or what it does." Jim told him about using the computer at the library, and what happened with the Internet light on the machine.

"That sounds pretty, you know, weird, Jim." Snickers reached out and took the drive. In the bar's dim lighting, he looked at it as closely as possible. "It doesn't, you know, look like anything special." He glanced up at Jim. "Okay, Jim. What's the, you know, story behind it? In general terms, you know? I don't want you to, you know, give away any secrets that you don't, you know, want to."

Jim had just been thinking about how much to tell the man. But, Snickers had always been accurate with his information, and Nicholas Turner trusted the man with his life, if need be. Word circulated about things like that in the private detective/security businesses around the city.

Jim suddenly let any doubts go, and told Snickers the whole thing. He interrupted the story only once, when Hazel arrived with drinks.

Snickers asked her to bring him another beer. "With a clean mug this time, you know?"

Hazel cackled at him as she walked away.

"You old harpy!" yelled Snickers. To Jim and Emily, he said, "See what I gotta, you know, put up with in this place?"

Jim and Emily laughed. Jim finished the background on the jump drive. Just as he wrapped the story up, Hazel arrived with a beer for Snickers.

The waitress put the mug down in front of Snickers. "Hank says ya gotta pay for this one, Snickers. Pay as ya go."

Snickers put a five-dollar bill on Hazel's tray. "Keep the, you know, change, Hazel. Thanks."

"Thanks, Snickers. You two want a refill?" she said to Jim and Emily.

Both thanked her and shook their heads. The waitress left.

Snickers took a sip of his beer and made a face. "Aw, crap! Hank gave me a, you know, *light* beer. Tastes like, you know, water!"

Jim sipped his drink. "So, what do you think, Snickers? Can you do anything with it?"

Snickers wrinkled his brow. "Yeah, Jim, I think, you know, I can get you some answers. Want me to, you know, take a look right now?" Snickers lifted a laptop computer from the booth seat beside him.

Jim shrugged. "It's up to you, Snickers. Just make sure that you don't have any Wi-Fi engaged on that thing."

Snickers snorted. "Jim. This isn't my first, you know, rodeo." Snickers powered up the laptop. "I'm disabling the, you know, Wi-Fi now. It's not really, you know, necessary. Hank doesn't offer, you know, Wi-Fi. But, some of the joints around here, you know, do, so I gotta turn it off." The man's fingers flew across the laptop's keyboard. "Okay, we're, you know, good to go. Give me the, you know, jump drive."

Jim passed the drive over to him.

Snickers plugged it in. His eyes were glued to the laptop's screen. "I have my, you know, laptop configured so that this drive is, you know, isolated. It will only run in one particular area of, you know, the computer, and maybe won't, you know, target the rest." He tapped a few keys. "Okay, you got what appears to be, you know, some kind of malware-type thing."

Jim was perplexed. And lost. He knew from Nicholas Turner that Snickers was a naturally gifted computer whiz, and now made his living working with them, as well as providing information as needed to various investigators and cops...for a price. Snickers was a former junkie, rehabilitated by Nicholas Turner, if the stories could be trusted. "What kind of malware, Snickers?"

"I dunno. It's, you know, encrypted. I've never seen this kind of, you know, encryption." He tapped a few more keys. "Oh, crap."

"What's wrong?" asked Jim.

"It's, you know, buried itself in the root directory," replied Snickers. "It's, you know, replicating itself. Every time I, you know, delete it, it pops right back in. I can't, you know, get rid of it." His fingers were flying over the keyboard. "Dammit!"

Emily looked concerned. "How about the data itself? Can you get anything from it at all?"

Snickers looked perplexed. "Haven't been able to, you know, get that far, Emily. What the flying fu...I mean, I'm, you know, sorry, Emily. What the hell is this?" Snickers finally gave up on trying to delete the file, shut the laptop, and looked at Jim.

"Jim, you didn't, you know, use that thing on any of your, you know, office computers, did you?"

Jim shook his head. "No. Only at the library. Especially after I found out that the money came from Esteban Fernandez, and everyone that's touched it has died."

"Yeah." Snickers was lost in thought. "Jim, this malware is, you know, determined to send a message to, you know, somebody. I don't have a clue who it, you know, might be, but you know as well as I know, that Esteban Fernandez is really bad news to, you know, this city."

Jim, remembering how he had helped Justice Security at Louie's boxing match when they first encountered Fernandez, nodded his agreement.

"I think I'll ease over to, you know, the library tomorrow...check 'em out. I can, you know, see if there's somebody weird, you know, hanging around. I'll ask around." Snickers pulled the jump drive out of the laptop and handed it back to Jim. "Damn. I hope, you know, that I can get that malware off of this thing. It's my, you know, favorite computer."

"If we get out of this in one piece, I'll gladly buy you a new one," assured Jim.

Snickers smiled. "Hey, that's great, Jim. Listen, if it's Fernandez, you know, doing this, you might want to think about, you know, letting Justice Security in on it. Word on the street is that, you know, they got a contract to go all out against him." Snickers shrugged. "Also, they got a first class, you know, computer hacker working for them. He's, you know, one of their partners. Dexter, or something."

Jim nodded. "Dexter Beck. I know him. He's a good man. Is he better than you, Snickers?"

Snickers shrugged. "I don't know, Jim. But they got, you know, lots better equipment than I can get to. They can, you know, kick ass if they have to."

"I know. I think I'll keep looking on my own right now, Snickers."

The nervous little man shrugged again. "Whatever you, you know, think, Jim. It's your carcass. I'll call you, you know, at your office tomorrow if I, you know, find anything."

"Thanks, Snickers. I'll try to squeeze in a conversation with you in between IRS agents," said Jim.

Snickers laughed. "You got them, too? So does, you know, Nicholas. Two of 'em, you know, showed up at his office today. Some kind of, you know, on the site audit. Took 'em about, you know, a couple of hours with Nicky. Everything was, you know, kosher, so off they went."

Jim shook his head. "I hope it's that easy for me tomorrow."

Chapter 5

The next morning, at nine o'clock, the IRS agents were the topic of discussion.

Every morning at nine, the Justice Security partners gathered in the situation room to discuss current and upcoming events. By doing this, they kept up with all company business in case someone else had to step in and take over quickly.

"Have you been monitoring them at all?" Joey Justice sounded concerned.

"Of course. You don't think I'm going to let those two wander around my computers without watching them, do you?" replied Dexter Beck.

"Sorry. Of course you wouldn't. Has there been anything suspicious?"

"Only with the occasional search, when no one is close to them."

"What are they searching for?"

Dexter consulted his notes. "Well, looks like they're typing in numbers for bank accounts. They're searching for any contact with a certain one."

"Really." Joey leaned forward at the conference table, and looked interested. "Any information on that number?"

"It's one used by Esteban Fernandez. But it's one that we know he uses to pay people that either work for him, or are on the take. A couple of times, they've tried searching the system by typing in Fernandez' name. No luck. The accounting system doesn't interact at all with our main system." Dexter leaned back. "I think we have a couple of moles, Joey."

Misty Wilhite looked very interested in the conversation. "I wonder what they're looking for? Payments to us from Fernandez?"

"Lemme go ask 'em, Joe." Louie Washington smiled his scary, I-want-to-hurt-something smile.

"Not yet, big guy." Joey smiled at his college friend. "Let's let them snoop around a bit more. Then, we might let Marcus ask them what they're really doing."

Marcus Moore was Justice Security's FBI liaison. Marcus had been instrumental in getting Justice Security's top secret contract with the United States Government, guaranteeing a large amount of money plus expenses to the security company...but, to earn the money, they had to bring down Esteban Fernandez. And the contract specified that it be done with full governmental deniability, of course, and no on-the-record help by any government agency. Expense money would be funneled to them on the Q.T. by Marcus. After the debacle that had been the *Wham!* nightclub, Marcus had been promoted to Section Chief at the Bureau's city office.

Jessica Queen stifled a yawn. "Do we have anyone physically watching them, Joey?"

Joey nodded at his partner. "Yes. Tony put the kids on them. I think the kids have ticked Tony off somehow."

"Or he could be testing their observation skills," added Megan Beck, Justice Security partner, and Dexter Beck's wife.

Joey nodded. "Could be, Megan. Let's let those two agents work today, then we'll do a little follow-up on them. Anyone have anything else?"

"SIR, I'M SAYING THAT I don't know when Mr. Dandy will be in. He's usually here by nine o'clock." Lena was looking exasperated. The two men in front of her reception desk were very pushy, and very arrogant.

"Can you tell us when he *will* be here?" asked one of the men.

Lena shook her head. "No, sir, I'm sorry. His secretary hasn't arrived, either. I'd be glad to take a message, and give it to him when he arrives."

Both men gave her cold, blank stares. Finally, the man that spoke said, "No. Thank you. We'll come back."

The men turned and walked away, toward the elevator. Lena overhead one of them say something, but all she understood was "Nicholas Turner". She made a face at their backs as she answered her ringing telephone.

"Jim Dandy Security. This is Lena. How may I help you?"

The voice on the other end said, "I'm lookin' for Emily Owens. She there today?"

"No, sir, I'm sorry. Emily hasn't made it in to work yet. May I take a message?"

There was a pause on the other end. "She not answerin' her cell phone, either."

Recognition came to Lena. "Turk? Is that you?"

"Yeah. How'd you know, Lena?"

"Please. How many men speak in monosyllables? Oh. Well. All of them. But none of them do it like you do, big man."

Lena could hear Turk chuckling.

"Lena, she broke our date last night. Now she not answerin' her cell. You know where she is?"

"No, Turk. She hasn't come in, and neither has Jim Dandy."

"That's weird. You call me when you hear something." It was an order, not a request.

Lena smiled. "I will, Turk."

They hung up.

Lena started to get a little uneasy. They were never late coming to work. And they always told her where they'd be.

Where *were* they?

"SEE? TAKE A LOOK." Snickers pointed his finger at the screen. "That's the, you know, address this damn malware wants to, you know, send its location to."

"Is that all that you've manage to decrypt?" asked Jim.

Snickers nodded. "Yeah, Jim, sorry, you know? That's it."

Jim Dandy sighed. He and Emily were having breakfast with Snickers in a booth at a small, diner-type restaurant, named 'Al's Big Eatery'. Al's was downtown, on Second Avenue. Snickers had called Jim early that morning and said that he had decrypted part of the malware, and wanted to meet with Jim, and Emily, that morning.

Jim frowned. "So, what does this mean, Snickers?"

Snickers rolled his eyes. "Lord save me from, you know, people that know nothing about, you know, web addresses!" He turned the computer back around so that the screen faced him. "Having the, you know, IP address that this thing sends its, you know, 'blip' to is big. Once I track down that, you know, IP address, all we have to do then is, you know, look it up and see who it belongs to." Snickers waved his hand in a 'there-you-go' gesture. "Then we can go ask them, you know, what the big deal is."

Emily smiled. "And if they're big, scary bad guys?"

Snickers smiled back. "Then we run, you know, like hell. Find a, you know, hole and pull it in after us."

Jim asked, "What did you mean by 'blip', Snickers?"

Snickers pointed at the screen with his hand. "A 'blip'...you know, it's a transmission of, you know, the IP address of the, you know, computer that the jump drive is plugged into. It downloaded onto the, you know, jump drive, along with the, you know, data that's there. The 'blip', you know, keeps sending its location to, you know, whoever is at the IP address I just showed you. It'll keep trying to, you know, send, until it does what it's, you know, supposed to. That's why it keeps, you know, replicating itself every time I, you know, delete it!" Snickers chuckled. "It even, you know, buried itself so deep, I tried to, you know, reformat the laptop's, you know, hard drive. The bug's still there."

Jim thought for a moment. "Can you mask your IP address somehow?"

Snickers thought about it. "Yeah, I probably, you know, could hide it. The problem is, you know, we can't be sure that this damned, you know, thing won't give out its real IP address anyway."

Jim smiled. "Want to try an experiment, Snickers? I'll gladly pay you for your time."

Snickers looked crookedly at Jim. "What do you, you know, got in mind?"

"Only if you want to risk it." Jim flashed his hundred-watt-smile again.

Snickers rolled his eyes, and then looked at Emily. "Does that, you know, shit-eating grin work on anyone?"

Emily laughed. "It works a lot more than you think it does. Mostly on females, though."

"I can, you know, believe it!"

Jim looked from one to the other. "Hey! Right here! Me!"

The other two laughed.

Finally, Snickers shrugged. "Why not? As long as I, you know, don't get shot or beat up, I'm game." He looked at Jim. "What's the plan?"

Jim told him, and both Emily and Snickers smiled with the simplicity of it.

"And the great part is that I won't have to buy you another laptop, once this thing does its job!" Jim smiled back at the two.

Emily peeked at her phone. Three missed calls, two from Justice Security, and one from Turk's personal cell. She would have to take a minute and call Turk, just so he wouldn't be worried.

She excused herself to go to the bathroom.

TURK PICKED UP THE phone. "Justice Security. This is Turk."

"Hey, babe. I can only talk a minute."

A surge of relief passed through the big man, but he made sure not to let it show. "Emily, where you been?"

"Were you worried?"

"Dumb question."

"I'm sorry, honey. We have something big going on right now."

"You with Jim?"

"Yes."

"You'll be safe, then."

"Jim will make sure of it, big man."

"Be careful, woman."

Turk could hear the smile in Emily's voice. "I will. See you soon."

They hung up.

Turk turned back to Louie Washington, who was standing at the side of Turk's desk.

Louie looked at his longtime friend. "Somethin' goin' on, man?"

Turk looked around to make sure that they were alone. "Emily. She say that her and Jim are on a big case."

Turk had, of course, let all of his bosses know through Louie and Misty that he was dating Emily Owens. At first, Joey didn't like it because of the rivalry between the two security firms, but Misty had reminded Joey that they had been close friends in college.

Misty also reminded him of something else. "Besides, Joey, you and I are engaged. I'm marrying you. Don't let your jealousy overtake you."

Back in college, Jim Dandy and Joey Justice had both fallen in love with Misty. But, to Misty, Jim had seemed just a little too...well-polished for her. She had known from the start that both men were devoted to her, but Joey just had a certain special something that she couldn't find in Jim. As a result of her choice, after college, Jim had opened a rival security company. Both companies helped each other out when needed, and Jim Dandy Security outbid Justice Security on a few government contracts, but Justice Security had prospered. Jim...well, Jim didn't do as well.

Misty had been right, so Joey had accepted it.

Louie nodded at Turk. "They okay?"

Turk looked at Louie. "She say they are right now."

"She know that we be comin' like the cavalry if they need us?"

Turk let a smile peek from the edges of his mouth. "She knows."

"Okay, then. Let's go over this Chicago expense sheet again. Man, I hate havin' expense account duty! We should just be able to give it to Accounting."

Turk grunted his agreement.

SNICKERS WALKED INTO the city's 12th District police station, and sat down in one of the visitor chairs. No one paid any attention to him.

He took his laptop from under his jacket, put it down on his crossed leg, and opened it. He let the machine search for the police station's wi-fi, and then he quickly deciphered the password. Once his machine was connected, he let the malware do its thing. Snickers verified that it was done by deleting it. When he could delete it without the malware replicating itself, he was done.

Snickers closed the laptop, tucked it back under his jacket, and left the building as unobtrusively as possible.

Jim and Emily were parked across the street, watching the building. They were sitting in a blue sedan, borrowed from a used car lot downtown. Snickers knew the guy that owned it, and the guy had let them borrow the car for some surveillance.

Snickers didn't wave or acknowledge the car in any way. He had performed his part of the plan, and was now heading to work. He was planning to wipe the hard drive, remove it from his laptop just to be safe, and replace it with a drive with more storage. Jim had agreed to pay for the new drive.

Emily watched as the man walked around the corner. "I hear that he's one of Nicholas Turner's best sources of information. If he's any kind of help to Nicholas like he's been to us, Nicholas is one lucky private investigator."

Jim's eyes were watching the entrance to the 12th District station closely. "He's sure been a big help to us."

Emily's gaze turned back to the station, too. "I wonder how long it will take?"

"If they're really desperate to get the information back, I'm guessing that it won't take long."

"I hope not, Jim. I could use a bathroom break."

"Hey, you want to call Lena and let her know that we're on a surveillance thing?"

"Sure." Emily pulled her cell from her purse and had just taken it out of sleep mode.

Jim said, "Look at this." He nodded toward a normal-looking, dark blue sedan. "That looks just like the one that I saw go into the parking lot at the library yesterday."

The sedan had turned into the parking lot at the police station. Jim lifted a pair of binoculars to his eyes. They had just purchased them at a downtown sporting goods store before they started this morning's trap. Jim could see the two men. Both were dressed in off-the-rack suits that screamed 'cop', and they seemed to be talking. Finally, one of the men took out a phone and made a call. He put the phone down a couple of minutes later. Then, the two men got out of the car and walked into the 12th District station.

"To borrow from Lewis Carroll, curiouser and curiouser," said Jim.

"Do you think those two were sent to intercept the drive?"

"I'm not sure yet, Emily. We'll see in a minute."

Less than ten minutes later, the two men exited the station. The taller man was looking all around him, as if he were memorizing the location...or looking for someone.

Jim watched without the binoculars. "Well, they know they've been made."

"How do you know?"

"They're looking around. It looks like they're trying to see who wants to see them."

"Have they seen us?"

"No. But that's only because the windows are so darkly tinted. You can bet they've seen the car."

"I think we should leave now, Jim."

"I think you're right, Emily."

Jim started the car and backed it out of the parking space. They pulled out onto the street on the opposite side of the parking lot, and sped away from the area.

Jim continued watching the rear view mirror to see if the two men followed, but it looked like he and Emily were in the clear.

Jim frowned. "Emily, there are only a few people that can act that fast in a situation. Big bad guys, like Fernandez or Giambini...or good guys, like government agents."

Emily shot a glance at her boss. "Which one do you think they were?"

Jim shook his head. "They were ballsy enough to go inside the police station. They probably asked questions. I'd say government agents. They had that smell about them."

"From what agency? And why?"

Jim shook his head slightly. "I don't know, Emily. But, I *do* know that we're in over our heads, and we need help. I'm going to have to swallow my pride, and go ask for some." He pounded his hand on the steering wheel. "*Damn* it!"

Chapter 6

"Whatever we did to piss Tony off, I think we should go apologize for it," said Patty Ferguson in a light whisper.

She and Brandon were on watch duty, assigned to the two IRS agents.

"Patty, have you noticed how many times they've performed a search using the 'Fernandez' name?" Brandon was studying the two men as they worked.

"Fernandez?" Patty was surprised. "Why would the IRS search for him?"

"I don't know. I think it's odd, though." He leaned closer to her so that he could whisper even lower. "They've also been searching for a series of numbers. I haven't been able to make out what the numbers might be, but they look like the same set every time. What's up with that?"

"Brandon, go tell Tony. I'll hold down the fort until you get back."

Brandon thought about it, then nodded. "You're right. He needs to know. I'll be right back." Brandon left the room.

Patty began watching the two men a little more closely.

Down the hall, Brandon found an empty office with a desk phone. He called Tony at the front desk and told him what he had noticed.

Tony was pleased. "Good eye, kid. I'll pass the word along upstairs. Keep watching them, and you two stay sharp."

Brandon hung up, used the rest room while he was up, and then returned to his post in Accounting.

Tony, meanwhile, called up to the fourth floor. He bypassed Turk, and dialed Joey's extension directly.

"This is Joey."

"This is Tony, sir. I have two things for you. The first is that I'm finally giving the thumbs-up for Brandon and Patty to go to plainclothes. They're ready."

"What convinced you, Tony?"

"That's number two, sir. Brandon reported that the two IRS agents are conducting computer searches using the same sequence of numbers each time.

He hasn't been able to see the numbers yet. Also, Brandon reports that they've done searches using the name 'Fernandez'. Should I go get them and bring them upstairs?"

Joey smiled. "Not yet, Tony. Give them until the end of the day. When they've finished, please escort them to my office."

"Yes, sir."

The two men hung up their phones.

Just as Joey took his hand away, there was a low knock on his office door.

Joey sighed. "Come in."

The door opened, and Turk leaned in. His massive shoulders filled the opening. "Boss, you got a phone call on line 2. I think you might want to take this one."

Joey tilted his head as he looked at Turk. *Turk never says that much. This call must really be something.* Out loud, he said, "Thank you, Turk."

Turk, frowning, left the office, and closed the door behind him.

Joey picked up the phone. "Joey Justice."

"Joey." The voice was a little breathless, but recognizable nonetheless. It was Jim Dandy.

"Hello, Jim. What's up?"

"I have to see you. Now, if you can. In your office."

"What's going on, Jim?"

"I've gotten hold of something big, and I can't do it alone. It's really dangerous. Joey, I need your help."

And there it was. Joey had waited for years to hear those words from Jim Dandy's mouth. He had dreamed of the day, and had even imagined the conversation that would follow.

"Joey, I need your help."

"Jim, do you remember, back in college, when we used to be best friends? And you blamed me for the fact that Misty chose me instead of you? We all invited you to join us as we formed Justice Security, but you wouldn't do it. Instead, you formed a competing security company, and have undercut us on more contracts than I can count. Do you remember all of that?"

"Yes, Joey, I remember. But can you help me?"

"Jim, if you're so good on your own, and if you think I 'stole' Misty's affections, I think you can get yourself out of trouble."

"But, Joey...!"

"Goodbye, Jim!"

That all ran through Joey's head in less than two seconds. He was surprised that it took that long, since he had it all memorized in his favorite daydreams.

But, what came out of his mouth was, "Come on in, Jim. I'll tell Tony to be expecting you. Let's see if we can fix this big thing."

"Emily and I are five minutes away, Joey. May we park in the garage?"

"Of course, Jim. Let me call Tony."

"Thanks, Joey!"

"You're very welcome, old friend." Much to Joey's surprise, he found that he meant it.

Joey pressed the disconnect button, and then let it come back up. He dialed the front desk.

"Front desk, this is Tony."

"Tony, this is Joey. Jim Dandy and his secretary will be here in less than five minutes. I want you to let them park in the garage, and then I want you to make sure that they get to my office quickly."

"Is there a problem that I need to know about?"

"I don't know yet, Tony. Jim says that he's clamped onto something big, and that he can't handle it alone. I'll let you know if it turns out to be something for us to worry about."

"Yes, sir."

THE ELEVATOR 'DINGED' in front of Turk. As per his standing instructions, his hand moved to the trigger of the semiautomatic pistol that was bolted to the underside of the reception desk. It was permanently aimed at the elevator, so that whoever was behind the reception desk could fire quickly if it was needed.

When Turk saw his friend Tony, and then Jim Dandy, and, finally, Emily, he took his hand off of the weapon and stood.

To Tony, Turk said, "He waitin' for you."

Tony nodded.

Turk held out his hand to shake with Jim. "Good to see you again, Jim."

Jim grasped the big man's hand and shook it. "You too, Turk."

Turk came around his desk, and wrapped his huge, muscular arms around Emily. He dwarfed her, but she was glad. In his arms, Emily felt safer than she'd ever felt. "You weren't worried, were you, Turk?"

A smile played around Turk's lips. "Naw. I knew Jim had ya covered."

Emily stood on tiptoe and kissed the big man. "I gotta go now, mister. Save it for later."

"Count on it, babe." Turk unwrapped his arms from her.

Tony looked at the two of them. "Emily, what in the hell do you see in this deviant bastard?"

Everyone laughed as Tony led the way to Joey's office.

When Tony heard "Come in!" after his knock, he opened the door and let Jim and Emily go inside. Then, Tony pulled the door shut, and then he continued to crack jokes with Turk, and wondered what was up.

Joey greeted Jim and Emily with a big smile. He came over to shake their hands. He gestured to the comfortable seating area. Seated in the office were all of the partners of Justice Security.

Misty Wilhite was seated in half of the love seat. Joey had risen from the other half when he welcomed his competitor. The couch contained Dexter and Megan Beck, and Louie Washington. Jessica Queen was seated in one of the comfortable armchairs. Two other armchairs were empty, awaiting Jim and Emily.

On the large glass coffee table, two trays rested. One tray held a big pot of coffee and several mugs, and the other tray contained various pastries and some small plates. All of the partners greeted Jim and Emily, and Joey invited them to sit down, and to help themselves to anything on the table.

Both took mugs of coffee, and settled back into their chairs.

After a bit of small talk, Jim came to the point. "Thank you for seeing us, Joey. Let me tell you about what we've run up against." He told them everything about the data on the jump drive, and what had happened with it all.

Dexter asked, "Jim, do you have any IRS agents at your offices right now?"

Jim looked puzzled. "Yes, I do. How did you know? Oh, that's right! They said that they were auditing all of the security firms in the city!"

Joey said, "We have two down in accounting right now. I have to say that they appear to be doing what they said they were going to do, but...they've been conducting computer searches for a sequence of numbers, and a name." He leaned forward to pour more coffee into his cup. "The number sequence is an offshore bank account known to be used by Esteban Fernandez. The name is, of course, Fernandez."

"Your story answers a lot of questions for us, Jim," said Misty. "We couldn't figure out why the IRS has suddenly taken an interest in those two things, unless they suspected us of taking payoffs."

"But, since I've got agents at my office, too, presumably doing the same thing, that means...," said Jim.

"...that someone ordered them to come. Someone with a lot of power, and the capability and willingness to use that power," finished Joey.

"Jim, that jump drive and that account information just became my favorite thing right now," said Dexter. Excitement was in his voice. "Megan and I can probably figure out what agency designed your little 'blip' program, and we can take it from there."

"Yeah, and guess what?" asked Megan. "You have two people here that are dying to meet this Snickers guy! Look at all he managed to accomplish with only a partially working laptop!" She shook her head in disbelief. "We have *got* to hire this guy!"

Joey stood, and walked behind his desk. "No, right now we have to ask questions." He picked up the phone and dialed. "Tony, this is Joey. Could you please escort those two IRS agents to my office, please? Yes, right away, please, and make sure they bring all of their belongings." He hung up the phone, and walked back around to the seating area. "We'll all hit these guys first, then we'll pay a visit to the ones in Jim's office."

TONY STROLLED INTO Accounting, and motioned to Brandon and Patty to join him.

Tony, using his military, don't-screw-with-me tone, said, "Mr. Gilbert, Mr. Purvis, I need you to gather your belongings and come with us, please."

Purvis, who had just been typing in the Fernandez name in the search bar again, jumped. He had been startled, and he quickly clicked on the 'minimize' button.

Gilbert looked up at Tony. "Our work isn't done."

Tony, the front point of a triangle completed by Brandon and Patty, said sternly, "Mr. Gilbert, I have no information about that. I only know what I was ordered to do." He looked into the IRS man's eyes. "I'll complete my orders, with or without cooperation from you two gentlemen."

Purvis had reached inside his suit coat with his right hand. Patty saw this, drew her sidearm faster than a gunslinger in a western, and said conversationally, "Freeze, mister."

Purvis froze.

"Pull your hand out. Slowly. And stand up." Patty's tone was very no-nonsense.

Purvis did as she asked.

Gilbert tried to defuse the situation. "He's no threat to you! We aren't armed!"

Tony put his hand on Gilbert's arm. "Mr. Gilbert. *Shut. Your. Pie. Hole.* Understand?"

Gilbert looked into Tony's eyes, and saw the lack of fear, and the determination to keep things under control. He also saw that he was very close to being physically uncomfortable. Gilbert raised his hands shoulder-high, and clamped his mouth shut.

"Against the wall, Mr. Purvis. Hands on the wall, spread your legs. Now!" Patty was insistent.

Purvis kept his hands raised, and put them against the wall.

Patty gestured for Brandon to pat him down. She had no intention of putting her weapon away until she was satisfied that Purvis was unarmed.

Brandon patted under the left side of the IRS agent's coat pocket. Something was there. Brandon reached into the man's pocket, and pulled out the item.

It was a phone.

Brandon continued to pat down the IRS agent thoroughly. He stood away. "He's clean, Patty. He was reaching for his phone."

Patty stood upright and holstered her weapon. "Thank you, Brandon. Mr. Purvis, you may step away from the wall now. I apologize. But you should not have reached inside your coat once Mr. Armstrong said you were to come with us. Things like that make a girl nervous." Her eyes twinkled above her sprinkling of freckles, and a smile played at the corners of her mouth.

"I'll try to remember that." Purvis' voice was full of sarcasm. He reached for the keyboard of the terminal he had been using.

"No, sir. You're done. Mr. Justice wants you two upstairs. Now. Please gather your belongings and bring them with you. You are not to touch anything else." Tony's voice was stern as he glared at Purvis. "Understood?"

Purvis nodded, and sneered. "Sure. I understand."

The two men gathered their belongings.

Tony said, "I'll lead the way. Brandon, Patty, I want you two to bring up the rear. If you see anything untoward from these two, bring them down."

"Yes, sir!" said Patty.

Brandon echoed, "Yes, sir!"

Tony turned and marched to the elevators. Once upstairs, he greeted Turk again, and led the way to Joey's office. He knocked, and opened the door when invited. He stood to the side, and gestured for the two men to enter the office.

"Tony!" called Joey. "Would you wait outside, please? We'll need your escort services again shortly."

"Yes, sir, we'll be right out here. Call if you need us. Please." Tony pulled the door closed.

Two hard, wooden chairs had been placed within the group setting. Joey indicated the chairs. "Mr. Gilbert, Mr. Purvis, please have a seat."

The two men shared a look, and then sat down.

Louie glared at the two men, as only Louie could. His look made both men nervous.

Joey began. "Gentlemen, as you may or may not know, we have many government contracts. Marcus Moore, the new Section Chief here in the city's FBI office, is our official government liaison, and we handle many, many sensitive cases. As a result of an attack on our building recently by an assassin working for Esteban Fernandez, we have begun taking extreme security precautions."

Joey gestured at the coffee and the pastries. "Please, help yourselves, gentlemen."

Neither man accepted any refreshment.

Joey nodded once. "By the way, let me introduce you to everyone here. This is my fiancé, Misty Wilhite." He continued around the circle until he came to Jim and Emily. "And this man is my main competitor in the city, Jim Dandy. The lady is his executive secretary, Emily Owens. We both seem to have the same problem. That problem is the sudden influx to our businesses by the IRS."

Gilbert began spluttering. "We've received orders from Washington...!"

Joey interrupted the man. "We know you received orders. We've both read them, and complied with the request. But we would like to know why you're conducting computer searches for Esteban Fernandez, and for this offshore bank account used by Fernandez." Joey rattled off the numbers.

Both IRS agents wore blank looks.

"Come on, guys. You were sent here and, probably, to Jim's office, specifically to search for those things. We know it, you know it. Would you like to tell us who ordered it?"

Louie leaned forward, imposing on the two men's space. His face still wore a fearsome glare. "Please," he said through clenched teeth.

Louie's intense look and clenched teeth did the trick.

Gilbert spilled all he knew. "Our boss got a call from somebody named Utley. Then he got another call from someone else. We don't know who, but he was saying 'yessir' an awful lot. When he hung up, he gathered up all the auditing agents, and gave them their assignments. All security firms in the city were to be audited, but mainly we were to search for those two things. If one of the teams got a hit, we were supposed to call in with it." He wiped nervous sweat off of his brow. "That's all we know, Justice. We were only doing what we were told."

Joey looked around at the group. "Does anyone else have any questions?"

No one spoke up.

Joey raised his voice a bit. "Tony!"

The office door swung open. Tony stood with his hand on his weapon.

"Tony, will you please escort these gentlemen out of the building?"

"My pleasure, sir."

To the IRS agents, Joey said, "Go back and tell your boss that I threw you out. Then tell him to call whoever called him, and to say that anytime that person wants to know something about my company, call me directly, because no one else will be allowed into the building. And please tell your boss to tell them that they can kiss my ass." Joey smiled. "Got it?"

Purvis only glared at Joey, but Gilbert nodded. "I got it." He actually smiled. "And I'll deliver it exactly as you've told me. I'd looking forward to seeing the boss's face when I do."

The two men stood, and Gilbert held out his hand. "No hard feelings, I hope, Mr. Justice."

"Not with you two, Mr. Gilbert. You take care."

Tony, Brandon, and Patty escorted the men out of the office, down to the lobby, and out of the front door.

Meanwhile, upstairs in Joey's office, the discussion continued.

"Now we know that something is up," said Joey. "Let's talk a while, before we go to Jim's office. What does everyone think, and where do we go from here?"

Louie made the first observation. "I don't think Fernandez is behind this. It hasn't got that...smell, for lack of a better word."

"I agree with Louie," added Dexter. "The money may have come from Fernandez, but I don't believe he's behind all of this."

Jessica spoke. "This feels like somebody made a total balls-up of a data leak. And now it has a government cover-up feel to it."

Megan and Misty both nodded their agreement.

Joey looked at his competitor. "Jim, what do you think?"

Jim stared at nothing for a minute. "Joey, I think we're in some deep, deep shit. It didn't take ten minutes for those two guys in the sedan to get to the 12th District Station after Snickers did what he did with his computer. If it's government, somebody is seriously corrupted, and that somebody has a lot of power."

There was a moment of silence, broken by Emily. "We could be killed, couldn't we?"

Joey laughed. "Emily, if Esteban Fernandez couldn't do it, some slick in an off-the-rack suit won't do it, either. We will take some precautions, however. Jim, who works face-to-face with clients at your office? Who's there every day?"

"Me. Emily. And Lena. That's it. Everyone else usually receives their orders from one of us at their homes. We can't afford something like this building that you have."

"Understood. I propose that the three of you stay with us. The fifth floor has available suites for just this purpose. You'll have complete privacy, and all the security that the building can offer." Joey tilted his head. "Hell, Jim, if you want, you guys can run your operation from here. We've got extra office space. You're welcome to it for the duration."

Jim couldn't believe what he was hearing, but he sure as hell wasn't going to turn it down. "Sounds good to me. It makes it easier to work on the case if we're right here, anyway," said Jim. "Emily?"

Emily nodded. "I like the idea, too." She was thinking of Turk. Turk didn't live in the building, but he would probably stay with Emily if she asked. She hoped.

Joey nodded. "Sounds good, then. Let's go clear the IRS pests out of your office, and move Lena, and your phone lines, here. Dexter can probably have the phones set up by the time we get to your office."

Dexter smiled. "Piece o' cake."

"Louie, do you mind going with Emily to the YMCA? We need to retrieve that material," asked Joey.

"I'd be glad to." Louie smiled at Emily. "I think we might even take Turk with us."

Chapter 7

Tony insisted on accompanying Jim and Joey. Neither man objected, so Joey decided to let Tony have some fun with the IRS agents.

Lena was surprised, to say the least, when her boss walked in with Joey Justice. Her surprise turned to interest when Tony entered behind them.

Lena was in her late twenties, and she caught herself staring at Tony much more than she should have. Tony, ever the gentleman, pretended not to notice.

"Lena," said Jim. "Where are the two IRS agents?"

"Yes, sir," replied Lena, with a far-off sound to her voice.

Jim looked at his receptionist, puzzled. Then he realized where she was looking. Jim turned to Joey and shrugged. "Lena!"

Lena jumped, startled. "Yes, sir!"

"Where are the two IRS agents?"

"In your office, sir."

Jim looked incredulous. "Why are they in my private office, Lena?"

"They showed me a piece of paper, and said it was a warrant. They said I had to let them in there."

"Joey, Jim, I have a request. May I please go and convince these intruders the error of their ways?"

"My God, Tony, do you have to sound like Louie?" Joey shook his head. "It isn't my call, it's Jim's. I don't have a problem with it, if Jim doesn't mind."

Jim smiled his hundred-watt smile. "Tony, I would be very grateful if you were to correct those men's behaviors. Be my guest."

Tony unbuttoned the buttons on each shirt sleeve, and began rolling them up. As he started rolling the second sleeve, he began walking steadily to Jim's office door. He opened the door quietly, and slipped inside. Once inside, he closed the door as silently as he had opened it.

Jim turned to Lena. "Lena, we're moving everything over to the Justice Security building. We only need the files for current cases. Everything else can be moved later, if it's needed. Also, once we're there, we'll be staying there.

I'm sorry to do that to you, but I've stumbled onto a big case, and it's very dangerous, so we're going..."

Jim was interrupted by a couple of loud crashes, along with the sound of skin on skin noises. They sounded like the fistfight noises from western movies – *smack! smack!* Then came a thud, followed by a second thud, then silence.

"We have to live in some guest suites in that building until the danger has passed. I'm sure we can find some escorts to go with you to get your things from home..."

Jim was interrupted again by his office door banging open. Tony had one hand in a firm grip on one of the men's collar, and his other hand firmly gripping the man's wrist and pulling it up toward the man's shoulder blades. Tony frog-marched the man, whose had some puffy areas on part of his face, to the front door of Jim Dandy Security. He kicked the door open, and literally threw the man out into the entry hall in front of the elevators. Tony turned and went back into Jim's private office. He came back out a few seconds later, frog-marching the second man in the same manner. This man's eye had some bruising, and his mouth was slightly bloody. Tony also threw this man into the hall, then followed him out and pressed the 'down' elevator button. When the elevator doors slid open, Tony picked one prone man up and threw him into the elevator, and repeated the process with the second man. Tony leaned in, pressed the first floor button, and came back inside.

"Oh, my God, I think I'm in love," said Lena, with a dreamy smile on her face.

Tony pretended not to notice.

THE MAN BEHIND THE counter at the Y was the same man that Emily had encountered the first time she went there.

"See that guy?" She pointed at the man for the benefit of Louie and Turk. "Last time I was here, he wouldn't let me go to the storage lockers. He said that it was because this was a men's facility."

Louie nodded. "It *is* a men's facility, Emily. But unless that locker is in the men's shower room, there's no reason that you can't go there."

Turk smiled at Emily. "Watch my man, Emily. You done got him fired up."

Louie adjusted his face to a scowl. "Let's go. Emily, you lead the way."

Emily smiled and strode into the reception area, with Turk and Louie following her. Both men towered over her, and she felt like a pop diva with an entourage.

The man behind the desk saw her coming, looked down, then looked back up at the two men accompanying her. His eyes widened slightly, and he drew in a sharp intake of breath, and exhaled.

"Ma'am," he began, "I told you the other day that..."

"Excuse me," interrupted Louie. "Are there any naked men in the storage locker area?"

"...you can't...huh?"

Louie repeated his question. "I said, are there any naked men in the storage locker area?"

Turk kept a straight face, but, inside, he was struggling.

The YMCA man was confused, and it showed on his face. He shook his head. "No, there aren't any naked men there."

Louie leaned forward, placing his hands on the reception desk. "So, why can't this lady retrieve something from her employer's locker?" Louie paused for emphasis. "And it really needs to be a *good* reason."

The man behind the reception desk swallowed audibly. "Be...because...my boss doesn't like women inside the YMCA."

"Hmph." Louis stood straight again. "*Not* a good reason. So, let me tell you what's gonna happen." He pointed at Emily. "*She* be goin' to the storage locker like her boss told her." He put his hand on the reception desk again and leaned forward. "Me and my man, here, are gonna stay right here with you, just to make sure that she ain't interrupted." Louie smiled, but the smile was frightening. "Is that okay with you?"

The man gulped again. "S-s-sure! Tha-that's great!"

Louie smiled wider as Emily retrieved the material from the locker. When the material was safely tucked inside her purse, she returned to the reception area, and nodded slightly at Louie.

Louie turned back to the man. "Now, see? That didn't hurt nothin', now, did it?"

"N-n-no, sir."

Louie pointed a finger at the man. "You have a great day, now, and thank you."

The trio left the building. They got into the car Louie had requisitioned from the Justice Security motor pool, and all three burst out laughing.

"Oh, my *God*!" said Emily, between giggles. "I thought that man was going to pee all over himself!"

Turk and Louie touched fists.

"Thank, m'man," said Turk.

Louie waved him off. "Don't think anything about it, man. You're my friend."

None of them noticed the nondescript, late-model sedan that began following them.

"LENA! DID YOU GET THE petty cash box?" called Jim.

"Why? Did you put some cash in it?" answered Lena.

Joey shared a look with Tony. "Nothing like a well-oiled machine," said Joey, loud enough so that only Tony could hear.

Tony, using the same low voice, said, "And this is nothing like a well-oiled machine."

Both men started chuckling.

Jim looked up and saw the two men laughing.

"Laugh away, you two. Believe it or not, we do a lot of good here." Jim was throwing files into a box.

"Jim, I know you do," said Joey.

Lena carried more files over to a box that was on the floor directly in front of the spot that Joey and Tony stood. She turned so that her back was to Tony. She bent over to put the files into the box, making sure that her rear was pointed at Tony.

That was all Joey could take. He went out into the elevator foyer and burst out laughing.

Tony took full advantage of the view, however.

And Lena knew he was watching. She stood up slowly, and turned around to face Tony. She reached up to Tony's face and pinched his cheek. "Oh, you are sooo cute! I could just...eat...you up!" Lena put her index finger in her mouth and slowly pulled it out. Then she winked at Tony.

Tony finally said, "Lena. Do you want something from me?"

Lena nodded her head as seductively as possible.

Tony took Lena's hands into his own, looked into her eyes, and said, "If we don't hurry up and get back to the building, we may not live long enough for that something to happen."

Lena let that thought process for a moment. She jerked her hands out of Tony's, and said, "Ohhhh!" with as much disgust as she could muster.

She did begin to move faster, though.

LOUIE TURNED THE CAR into the drive leading to the underground garage at the Justice Security building. The sedan drove just past the building, and parked in front of the coffee shop across the street.

Mark Haase, the evening shift grunt that covered the desk in Tony's absence, noted the sedan, mainly because it stopped so abruptly and parked. And nobody got out of the car.

When the elevator stopped at the lobby level, Louie, Turk, and Emily got out of the elevator car and came over to check in with Mark.

"Anything goin' on, Mark?" asked Louie.

"Yeah, I think you guys were followed." Mark pointed to the sedan parked in front of the coffee shop, and told them what it had done.

"And the guys are still sittin' there?" asked Louie.

"They are," responded Mark.

Louie thought for a minute. He nodded to himself. "Put a camera on their ass, Mark. Record everything they do. Take pictures of their faces, and give them to Dexter. He got some killer face recognition software, and we can hook into the government records, too. Let's see who these punks are." He tapped on the desk twice. "Let me know if they do anything besides go get coffee." He turned to the other two. "Come on, let's go see what Dexter's doin'. Turk, you can go back to your desk if you want, or you can come with us."

Emily smiled shyly at Turk.

"I be comin' with you, boss."

JIM WAS PEEVED. "LENA, are you through screwing around? We've got to go!"

Lena took a huge breath and released it in a sigh. She looked around the office, nodded her head, and said, "I think we've got everything we'll need, Jim."

Joey was carrying the final box as they left the Jim Dandy Security office. Jim stopped and locked the doors behind him. *Man! I sure hope this crap ends soon. I'm going to miss my office.*

On the way down in the elevator, Lena inched as close to Tony as she could. Tony stared straight ahead.

Joey and Jim were in the back of the elevator. Joey nudged Jim, and nodded toward the two people in front. Jim looked at Lena. He shrugged and made a face, as if to say, "I don't know".

They had decided to retrieve Jim's car, and Joey had assigned a grunt to return the borrowed car to the car dealership, with a couple of hundred dollars to give to the dealer for allowing Jim to borrow the car. Joey told Tony to drive the company car back to the building, and to take Lena with him. Tony was to deliver Lena to Emily. Joey pulled Tony off to the side.

"Tony, I'm sorry. I have to talk to Jim, and the best way to do that is alone in the car. I'm sorry that I have to let her ride with you."

Tony looked at Joey and slowly winked his eye. That meant that Tony didn't mind, which was a relief to Joey. "Joey, don't worry about it. She's cute. And I have no doubt that she's interested in me. That makes things a lot easier."

Joey smiled, and patted Tony on the back. "You're off duty once you've done what I asked."

Tony smiled and said, "Yes, sir."

Tony and Lena got into the company car and drove back to the Justice Security building.

Joey had loaded the last box into the company car, so he climbed into the passenger seat of Jim's car empty-handed.

"Ready, Joey?"

"Anytime."

Jim started the car and they began driving.

"So, Joey, I know you want to talk to me, or you never would have dumped Lena onto Tony."

Joey smiled. "Actually, Tony thinks she's cute. I think he may try to score."

"Oh, dear God! First Emily, now Lena! What the hell, Joey?"

Joey shrugged. "Not doing it on purpose, Jim." He laughed. "Tony is really all business when he has that uniform on. But Lena doesn't know she's got a tiger by the tail."

"I think Tony might be the one with the tail in hand at this point, Joe."

Both men laughed.

Joey finally started talking about what he wanted to talk about.

"Jim...you know that Misty and I are engaged now, right?"

"Hell, I think the whole city knows it."

"Are you okay with it?"

Jim started to give a flippant reply, but he saw real concern in Joey's face when he glanced over at him. He changed his answer to the truth. "Yeah, Joey, I'm okay with that. She loves you, not me."

"No, Jim, that isn't true. She does love you. Just not the way you want her to love you." Joey looked at his old college friend, took a deep breath, and dove into what was bothering him. "We *all* still love you, Jim. You're still our friend. That's why we dropped everything and came running to help. It's what you would do for us, if we needed it."

"I think you do need it, Joey, what with Fernandez being a constant threat, and wanting to kill you so badly. And that's all the time, man! Do you know how much money is on your head right now?"

Joey smiled as if he knew something that Jim didn't. "I have a good idea, Jim. Part of the money simply it isn't there anymore, though."

Jim looked over at Joey. "What happened? What money isn't there?"

"I can't talk about it, Jim."

"Why can't you talk about it?"

"National security."

"You're kidding! What is it, really?"

"National security."

"Okay. National security. Explain."

Joey looked at Jim with a serious look. "Jim, this can't go any further. I could get into trouble for even telling you any of it."

"Joey. You know I'm the last person you have to worry about talking."

"I know. I just had to hear you say it." Joey took a breath. "Okay, after the nightclub thing…"

"You mean *Wham!*, don't you?"

Joey nodded. "After that, Marcus got promoted to Section Chief, and was placed in charge of the FBI office here in the city. The government decided that Esteban Fernandez was a threat to National Security, and we were given an exclusive contract. We are to bring down Fernandez, with all the quiet taxpayer money that it takes for expenses, and a hefty chunk of change when it's done. Marcus is our unofficial 'lubricant'…as Louie puts it, Marcus 'greases things up so that we can sliiiide right in.'"

Jim looked at Joey with his mouth wide open. "You have *got* to be kidding me!"

"Did you see anything on the news this past November about a gang war on the east side of Chicago?"

Jim nodded. "I did. Weren't over a hundred people killed from that?"

"It wasn't a gang war. Fernandez had tried to take over Chicago's drug trade. We found out about it, and put a stop to it." Joey paused for a moment. "I *did* get a submarine out of it, though."

"Get ouuuutt!"

Joey smiled. "Fernandez used a submarine in Lake Michigan to smuggle in men, weapons, and drugs. He abandoned it after we kicked his ass." Joey paused again. "I was able to punch him, and that was the most satisfying punch I've ever thrown in my life."

Jim looked puzzled. "So, why didn't you bring him in?"

"Felix Juarez snuck up behind me and bashed my head with the butt of his gun."

"And how are *you* still alive?"

"One of the people helping us shot Juarez in the leg, and another was shooting at Fernandez. They bailed in the submarine. It was found floating in Superior, and Fernandez was long gone. So, I took it, and it's docked down at the bay now."

"Joey, that is the ultimate cool!"

"It is pretty cool, isn't it?"

They rode quietly for a few beats.

Jim broke the silence. "Joey, I know that I let Misty come between us...and between Louie and Dexter, too. I was wrong to blame you. Hell, I was wrong to blame anybody. She loves you, Joey, and I had to accept that. It was a bitter pill, but I finally swallowed it." He paused. "I'm trying to say that I'm sorry."

"You weren't the Lone Ranger, there, Jim. I let it affect our friendship, too. Hell, I think we'd all welcome you even now, if you wanted to join up with us. I know I would. And, I'm sorry, too. I've missed you."

It was quiet inside the car for a few beats. Jim broke the silence. "We're not gonna, like, hug or anything, are we?"

Joey shook his head. "No, I think we can safely skip that."

JIM PARKED HIS CAR in the underground garage. He and Joey rode the elevator upstairs, to the lobby.

Tony was standing beside Mark behind the front desk. Louie was leaning against the desk, and they all seemed to be watching one of the monitors.

"What's up, guys?" asked Joey.

Louie explained about the sedan across the street. He finished the story with, "Dexter's got their pictures, and he's running them right now. Maybe we'll know something soon."

"And they haven't left the car?"

Louie shook his head.

"Who do you think they are?" asked Jim.

"Government," said the other four men in unison.

Jim chuckled. "My thinking, too. But how did they tip to the Y, I wonder?"

"Could be anything," answered Louie. "Maybe they camped out at the bus station and the train station. Maybe even the docks. Who knows?"

Jim nodded. "Yeah. And all it took was some known members of a security company or two to confirm what they suspected."

Joey turned to Jim. "Jim, we aren't helpless, and neither are you. If we do what we talked about in the car...hell, even if you don't, we can sic some serious muscle on whoever is doing this." He turned back to the front window. "They don't realize what a huge can of hornets they're about to open."

Chapter 8

The front desk phone rang, and Mark answered it.

"Front desk, this is Mark."

"Mark, this is Dexter. Is Louie there?"

"Yes, he is, and so are Tony, Joey and Jim Dandy."

"Oh, well, in that case, let me talk to Joey."

"Sure." Mark held the phone receiver out. "Joey, it's Dexter."

Joey took the phone. "Hey, brother, whatcha got?"

"It's pretty big. You want to come down here, or should I come up?"

Joey thought for a moment. "We'll come down. Save you some time." He handed the phone back to Mark, who hung it up.

Joey turned to Louie and Jim. "Dex has something, so we're going down."

The two men nodded, and followed as Joey began to walk.

Joey spoke over his shoulder. "Tony, I told you – you're off duty. Go home."

"No, sir," Tony called out.

Joey shook his head as he walked. "Damn hardheaded jarhead."

"I heard that," called Tony.

"You were supposed to!"

Joey started laughing as the three men got into the elevator.

"THIS IS WEIRD, GUYS," said Dexter. He and Megan were sitting side by side at two different computer terminals.

Joey, Jim, and Louie were standing behind them.

On Dexter's screen were the government-issued ID photos for the two men sitting in the sedan outside. On Megan's screen were the same two men, but the photos were slightly different.

"Okay, on my computer, these guys are listed as FBI men...Agents Johnson and Smith. On Megan's computer, they're listed with the Treasury Department, but with different names...Carmichael and Whitman."

"Yeah, and we can't figure out which is which," added Megan.

Dexter's computer beeped. "Uh, oh. We've got a third match." The ID photos popped up. These were slightly different than the other two. "These are Secret Service. Hemby and Slater."

Megan's computer beeped. "And another. Capitol Hill. Aides to some Senator. Trammell and Goodwin."

Joey's arms were crossed as he looked from screen to screen. "Jeez. Who are these guys?"

"I think we should go ask 'em," said Louie. "*Not* politely."

"I have a better idea," said Jim. He smiled his hundred-watt smile. "Let's fire up the jump drive and see what happens."

As the thought went through each head, they all began smiling.

AGENT JOHNSON'S CELL phone rang. He answered, "Johnson." He listened for a few minutes, and said, "Yes, sir." He ended the call.

To Smith, he said, "The Justice Security building. The tracker just went off."

"Do you think we ought to try this?" asked Smith.

"Sure, why not?" replied Johnson.

The two men climbed out of their car.

MARK SPOKE FIRST. "HERE they come, Tony."

"I see them." Tony picked up the phone, and dialed the computer room.

Dexter answered. "Computer room, this is Dexter."

"Dexter, this is Tony. Tell Joey that the two guys are coming inside."

"I'll be damned. Hold on, Tony." Dexter covered the phone, but Tony could still hear his muffled voice telling the others. After a pause, Dexter came back on. "Tony, stall them. We're on our way up."

"Yes, sir." Tony hung up. "Mark, we're to stall them until they get up here."

"That's not a problem. We can do that all day long."

The two men pulled open the front doors just as Mark finished his remark. They walked to the reception desk. Johnson pulled out his FBI badge and ID, and displayed it for Mark and Tony.

"I'm Agent Johnson, and this is Agent Smith."

Tony stood with his arms crossed. "Yes?"

"We'd like to ask a few questions."

Tony stood firm. "Concerning?"

Johnson smiled a condescending smile. "We'll ask the questions."

Agent Smith was walking around the side of the front desk.

Mark said to Smith, "Sir, you might want to come back around to the front."

Smith looked at Mark. "I'll do as I please."

A voice came from behind Smith. "No, you'll do as *I* please, gentlemen." Joey walked up to the men, followed by Louie, Dexter, Megan, and Jim. "Right now, I want you to do what Mr. Haase told you to do."

Johnson looked at Joey. "And you are...?"

Joey leveled his eyes at Johnson's. "My name is Joey Justice. Can you tell me which name you're using today?"

"Sir, the names he gave were Johnson and Smith." Tony's face was blank as he reported.

"Sure it wasn't Carmichael and Whitman?"

Johnson's eyes widened a bit.

"Or maybe it was Hemby and Slater?"

Johnson's eyes narrowed. He was angry.

Joey snapped his fingers. "I know! It was Trammell and Goodwin!"

Johnson's jaw clenched. "What kind of game is this, Justice?"

"That's funny. I was about to ask you the same question. And if Mr. Smith doesn't get back around to the front of this desk, we'll put him back ourselves."

Smith hadn't moved at all, and was still standing to the side of the desk. Mark was keeping his eyes on the man. Everyone else's attention was on Johnson.

"Justice, we're Federal agents. That's all you need to know. And we're going to ask you some questions."

"Bullshit." Joey was beginning to get angry now.

Smith hadn't noticed that Mark was watching him. He began moving his right hand under his coat.

Mark drew his sidearm faster than Smith could believe. It was pointed directly at his face. "You might want to put that hand back where it was. Now, please."

When Mark drew his weapon, so did Tony. But Tony's weapon was pointed at Johnson. "Sir, I will kill you."

Joey smiled at Johnson. "You and I both know why you came in here. We have that jump drive. We're keeping it. And we're going to find out who is giving you your orders, and who is taking payoffs from Esteban Fernandez. When we find out, you'll all go down." He moved so that his face was an inch from Johnson's. "Count on it. Now get out, or be carried out."

Johnson held the gaze with Joey for a few seconds. "You'll pay for this one, Justice."

Joey shook his head. "No, but I might *get* paid for this one. Out. Last time I'm telling you."

Louie moved up closer to Johnson, and so did Dexter. Jim and Megan fanned out and faced Smith.

Finally, Johnson broke the stare. He spoke to his partner. "Let's go."

The two men walked casually to the front door and out. They crossed the street, got into their car, and drove away.

A few minutes later, Patty Ferguson came through the front doors.

"Did you have enough time, Patty?" asked Joey.

Patty smiled and nodded. "Almost. I got the tracker on under the car, but I didn't have time to get inside the car to put in the transmitter. I should have taken Brandon with me."

Joey shrugged. "That'll have to be enough for now. Good job!"

Patty beamed. "Thank you, Joey."

Joey turned to Dexter. "Okay, let's go activate that thing, and find out where they're going." To Tony he said, "You're off duty, Tony. That's an order."

"Yes, sir."

As the group walked back to the elevators, Joey told Jim in a very low voice, "The only thing a damn jarhead understands is an order."

Jim laughed.

SMITH WAS DRIVING.

Johnson was on the phone. "Yes, sir...no, sir, he openly said that he had the jump drive." He listened. "He said that they'd find a way to track whoever was receiving payoffs from Fernandez, and would bring them down." He listened. "No, sir, I don't have any idea what to do at this point. He has the information, and I don't have a way to muscle it out of him." Listened. "No, sir, no leverage at all. He doesn't scare." He listened again. "Yes, sir, we'll wait to hear from you." He disconnected the call and put the phone in his jacket. "He wants us to just hang loose. He has to think of a way to penetrate Justice Security's stubbornness."

"Why can't we just blow up the building or something?" asked Smith.

"Don't be stupid. Deniability, remember?"

Smith banged his hand on the steering wheel. "*Shit!*" he said forcefully.

The two men drove in silence for a few minutes.

Johnson said, "Let's go back to the YMCA. We'll question the clerk."

Smith nodded.

When they arrived, they parked their car in the parking lot located beside the building. As they began to get out of the car, a small device in Smith's pocket began beeping.

Smith took the device out and looked at it. "Son of a bitch. We've got a bug!" He began moving the device around the car. It became a solid beep on the passenger side of the sedan, underneath the rear door. Smith reached under the car, and pulled out a tiny tracking device.

"Well, I will be damned!" said Johnson. "When did they have time to do that?"

"Doesn't matter," replied Smith. He dropped the tracking device onto the ground and crushed it under his shoe. "They know we're here now. We can't kill the damn clerk."

"No point going in, then. He won't know anything."

"Let's go back to base."

THE GROUP AT JUSTICE Security watched as the tracker disappeared from the computer screen.

"They must have found it," said Megan.

"At least we probably saved the YMCA clerk's life," said Jim.

"Yeah, but we lost them." Joey shook his head. "I guess it's time to call Marcus in."

Chapter 9

At that moment, Marcus Moore was on a plane. The plane was a flight from Washington, D. C. to the city.

Marcus wished he were anywhere else.

What is it about me and planes? Every time I'm on one, it seems like a storm comes up, or turbulence, or some damn thing!

Marcus had been at Quantico with Tory Masterson, getting him all signed up for the training he would have to receive before becoming an FBI agent. Tory was a former Chicago cop that had gone above and beyond on the recent Chicago incident with Fernandez, and Marcus had given Tory the opportunity to join the FBI. He had taken it eagerly, and would be finishing his training before coming to the city to work for Marcus. Tory had gotten his wife and baby settled into an apartment in the city, and then accompanied Marcus to Quantico.

Marcus wished he had stayed at Quantico, and never even thought about a plane ride.

He had been throwing up all through the flight, as the plane made its convolutions through the air. He had filled three airsickness bags, and was about to fill a fourth.

His phone was in his pocket, switched off.

I don't think God wants me on planes, he thought, as he filled up a fourth bag.

JOEY LISTENED AS HIS call went to voicemail. *Dammit, Marcus!* "Marcus, this is Joey. It's urgent. Please come to the building when you get this message. Hurry."

The group had come up to the fourth floor, and settled into the situation room. It was late evening, and everyone was thinking about dinner. The discussion turned to the two faux FBI men, and what could be done about them.

"Voicemail again?" asked Misty.

Joey nodded. "I think I'll try the office, and leave a message there, too. Maybe they can tell me where I can find Marcus. Excuse me, folks." Joey stepped over to a corner of the room.

Misty and Jessica had shown the office setup they had created for Jim to operate his business to Emily and Lena. Both were satisfied with the setup, and decided that they had everything they needed to continue operations as normally as they could, under the circumstances. Jim hadn't seen it yet, but Emily assured the Justice Security ladies that it would be sufficient.

Jim, Emily, and Lena had never seen the situation room, and they were suitably impressed.

Jim had offered a comment. "No wonder I could never outdo you guys! This setup is spectacular!"

Turk remained at his desk, and had said that he would wait for Emily. Tony had called up to tell Lena that he would go home and clean up a bit, and then come back and take her to dinner, if she'd like to be seen with him. She said that she would love to go.

With Joey on the phone, Jim took the time to offer the same apology he had given to Joey on the ride to the building that afternoon.

Misty smiled demurely. "Thank you, Jim. I know that it was hard on you. But I love Joey so much! I can't imagine being without him!"

Jim smiled back. "Misty, if it makes you happy, then I'm happy, too. Louie, Dexter...I hope we can all be friends like we used to be."

"Maaaann," said Louie, "Who says we ever stopped?"

Dexter chimed in. "Yeah, Jim, what the hell? Do you think we drop everything for people all the time?"

Jim nodded. "Yeah. I do."

"Well, okay, we do. But not like we do for friends," said Dexter. "We're here for you, and we're glad you're here."

"I've only spoken to you a few times, but I'm very pleased that you're here," added Jessica. "Maybe now we can begin concentrating on working together instead of outbidding each other."

Jim leaned forward. "You know, Jessica, Joey said something like..."

"Okay, Marcus is on a plane somewhere between here and D. C.," interrupted Joey. "They'll give him a message, too, in case he misses his voicemail." He plopped down into his chair. "They also said they'd do some checking on our two visitors."

Misty touched Joey's arm. "Joey, I think we should stop for the night, and let these people settle into their rooms. None of us have had dinner."

A knock came from the door. Everyone turned to see Tony Armstrong standing there, dressed in dark slacks and a polo shirt.

Tony, arms at his sides, looked at Lena. "I'm sorry to interrupt, but if you folks can spare Lena, I thought I'd take her to Kenzie's for dinner."

Lena smiled. "Tony, I would love dinner at Kenzie's." She stood, and walked over to Tony. She stood on tiptoe, kissed Tony on the cheek, and linked her arm in his. "Good night, everyone. Don't wait up."

Tony blushed beet red.

Joey, fighting hard to keep a straight face, waved the couple off. "Go on. Have a good time." Under his breath, he said, "Jarhead."

"I heard that," Tony retorted, as he and Lena left.

Misty smiled at the two men. "Jim, would you and Emily like to see your rooms now?"

"Sure," said Jim.

"Sounds good to me," added Emily. "I'd like to freshen up a little before dinner."

"Hey, if you need anything that isn't in the room, I can help you out there," said Megan.

"*Please* take some of her stuff," Dexter said. "I have zero room on our bathroom counter now. You could take one of everything, and I *still* wouldn't have any room."

Megan punched his arm. "Ass."

Dexter smiled at her. "But I'm yours."

Megan smiled back. "And I'm yours, sweet husband."

"Ya'll wanna let me go throw up now? I think I got too much sugar in my system from all that." Louie was shaking his head.

Everyone laughed.

Jessica said, "I'm famished. If everyone is finished whispering sweet nothings, I suggest that we show Jim and Emily to their rooms, and then we all meet in the cafeteria in twenty minutes."

Everyone agreed to Jessica's plan.

"WOW! ALL THIS SPACE? Just for me?" Jim was impressed.

Joey looked sheepish. "Actually, Jim, we gave you the smallest suite. The fifth floor has smaller apartments than the sixth. Jessica actually chose to live on this floor. You, Emily, and Lena will be the only other current tenants. Turk could live here if he wanted to, and so could Tony, but they both chose to live outside the building. Understandable, of course."

The suite had a kitchen/dining room, a living room, a spacious bedroom with a king-sized bed, and a large bathroom, with both a Jacuzzi tub and a separate shower stall. It was furnished.

"Now, if you decide to do what we talked about, you can bring in your own furniture. The janitorial staff also will clean your rooms and change your sheets as you specify, unless you want to do it yourself. None of us on the sixth floor allow Janitorial into our rooms. I think Jessica does occasionally, but not very often. The option is there, if you want it."

"Are you guys trying to seduce me with all of this?" asked Jim.

Joey shrugged. "Yeah, I guess so. And I won't lie to you about the danger. You know as well as we do that the threats from Fernandez are real. The government would not have offered that contract if they weren't."

Jim looked at Joey. "Does the offer extend to Emily? To Lena? And what about the rest of my people? There aren't a lot, granted, but I don't want to leave them without jobs."

Joey smiled. "The offer to live inside the building doesn't extend to Emily or Lena. It's reserved for partners and the executive secretary. We would all be sharing Turk. But, if you come in as a partner, and the other person I have in mind comes in as a partner, it may be too much for one person. At that point, Emily would be first in line for the job. As for Lena, she can have her choice of working in the secretarial pool or as a plainclothes operative, if you think she can do it. Accounting, HR, or even the computer lab would be open to her, as well. As for your agents, Jim, you know we always need people. They will have jobs with us, if they choose to accept them."

Jim nodded. "You said another person is being considered. May I ask who that might be?"

Joey shook his head. "I can't say anything right now. We've offered this person jobs with us before, and the jobs have been turned down. If you come in as a partner, we'll fill you in on this person. It looks like the only way to get this one into our ranks is to offer a full partnership. It would be well worth it just to have this person." He looked at Jim. "Are you in a hurry? I have an idea that I'd like to talk to you about. It's something that would keep Emily as an executive secretary, and would still leave you autonomous."

Jim raised his eyebrows. "Sounds cryptic. Tell me."

Joey told him, and when he finished, both men were quiet.

Jim finally said, "That sounds really interesting, Joey."

Joey nodded. "I think it's time, and you're just the man to do it. If I can get this other person, I would hope that you would have help, if needed."

"Mind if I think about it a little? Maybe talk to Emily?"

Joey waved his arm. "Sure! But swear her to secrecy, Jim. Especially with that last part. I don't want the world to know. Not just yet, anyway."

"You got it, Joey. And I'll let you know soon."

MISTY STOOD CLOSE TO Joey in the cafeteria line. Her voice was very low. "Did you talk to him about it?"

Joey's voice was equally low. "I did. He's interested. Concerned for his people."

Misty smiled at her fiancé. "Just like you, if the positions were reversed."

Joey nodded. "You're right. Jim and I are a lot alike in a lot of respects. I wouldn't still like him so much if we weren't."

"But you have me. Jim has a slight...infatuation, maybe...with himself. Or, maybe not. I don't know, Joey. But I do know that it's you that I fell in love with, and it's you that I want to spend the rest of my life with."

Joey smiled. "And I'm the luckiest man in the world." He winked at her. "Just ask me."

Misty slapped him on the arm.

Just as everyone had settled down to the table, Joey's phone rang. He looked at it, and then looked at the group. "It's Marcus." He answered. "Marcus. Finally. How was the flight?"

"Oh, my dear God! I'm telling you, God does not like to have me in the air, Joey!"

Joey chuckled. "How many bags did you fill this time?"

"Four."

"Only four?" Everyone at the table began laughing.

"Yeah, and the fourth one was faulty. It fell apart. Messy, and I don't wanna talk about it."

"It fell apart? Ewwww!" Everyone at the table began laughing harder.

"Why am I hearing laughter? Do you have me on speakerphone?"

"Nope. Everyone knows where you were, and I'm just repeating what you've said."

"Oh, that's just great! As if I wasn't embarrassed enough!"

"Sorry, buddy. That's what friends are for!"

"What's going on? The office said you had called, and I got your voicemail, too."

"It's long and complicated. Jim Dandy has stumbled onto some important information, and we're working it with him. I don't want to go into it on the phone."

"I can't come tonight, Joey. I smell like...well, you know what I smell like. I need to go home and shower, and go to bed."

"That's fine, Marcus. Can you be here at nine o'clock tomorrow for the morning meeting?"

"I don't see why not."

"Great. We'll see you then."

"Okay. Bye, Joey."

"Bye, Marcus." Joey disconnected the call. To the group, he announced, "Marcus will join us for the nine o'clock meeting."

Everyone nodded or acknowledged Joey's announcement.

The rest of the evening was spent eating dinner, reminiscing with each other, catching up on things that had been missed, and renewing their friendships.

Chapter 10

"So these two guys came up with four different government IDs?" asked Marcus incredulously.

Dexter began typing on a keyboard in front of his place at the conference table. "Sure did. Here they are."

The four different ID photos came up on four of the wall mounted monitors in the situation room.

Marcus studied them carefully. Finally, he shook his head. "I don't know them at all, but I'll sure get the office working on it. Dexter, can you arrange to send those four IDs to the office?"

Dexter nodded once as he began to type. "I can."

Marcus picked up the landline phone in front of him. "I can use this?" he asked Joey.

Joey nodded.

Marcus dialed. "Henning, this is Marcus. I need to speak to Jackson." He waited. "Jackson, this is Marcus. I'm at Justice Security. They've ID'd a couple of men with multiple government IDs. I need to know who they are, and where these IDs come from. The pictures are being emailed to you as we speak." He looked at Dexter, who nodded. "You should have them now. Start tracking these guys down. I want everything you can get your hands on." Marcus disconnected the call and put the phone back into his pocket. "That should get something going."

"Thank you, Marcus." Joey put his elbows on the table. "I believe these two are bad news. Very bad news."

"I think you're right." Marcus shook his head. "This is something, all right. You don't believe these two are working for Fernandez?"

Jim spoke up. "No. I believe they're working for whoever Fernandez is paying off. This mystery person doesn't want anyone to know he's taking payoffs, and has the power to back that up."

Louie said, "I believe somebody should go find this Utley guy and beat it out of...I mean, *question* him."

Joey smirked. "You volunteering to fly out there, big guy?"

Misty looked shocked. "Joey, you can't let him go alone!"

"I'll go with him. If we have time, I need to divert to Los Angeles, and find out if Charlie Li is coming back to work." Jessica frowned. "I haven't heard from him since he married that Hollywood knob jockey." Charlie Li had married famous movie actress Carly Stewart a few weeks earlier. The job had been to guard the woman, who was a notorious drunk and a drug user, from any would-be attackers. Charlie had taken over the job from Jessica, who had been called to Chicago to help with the Fernandez mission. Ms. Stewart had proclaimed her love for Charlie, and the two had gotten married after knowing each other for a week. Charlie had not left the actress's side since.

"I'd love for you to come, Jessie, but I'm not sure that we'll have time for Los Angeles, and Charlie's narrow ass," said Louie. "We may have to come back here fast."

"We can take the jet, and see what happens, Louie. If we have time, I do want to see Charlie...and kick that drunken bitch's ass. As if she'd feel it."

Everyone around the table chuckled.

Joey said, "Jessica, don't you think Charlie is happy with his new wife?"

"His bloody *knob* is happy. Dunno about the rest of him," quipped Jessica.

Everyone laughed again.

Marcus said, "Louie, use your national security credentials if you have to. This *does* pertain to the Fernandez contract, so there won't be any problem with it. Threaten the guy with Guantanamo."

"I'll threaten the guy, all right. Don't know 'bout Guantanamo."

Marcus turned to Dexter. "Dex, we need to know who owns that account."

"Oh, we're on it, Marcus. Trouble with hacking into some of those secret banks is that they hack back. I'm assuming that we don't want them to know we're the ones doing the hacking, so I'm taking precautions. But the precautions cost us speed."

"Can you make up time? I mean, can brute force help? A full-frontal computer attack?" asked the FBI man.

Megan shook her head. "They expect that kind of attack. We have to sneak in without being detected. That takes time, and there's no other way around it."

Dexter took Megan's hand. "She's right. We'll get it, and we'll get it quietly. We can't guarantee that they won't know we have it, but we can guarantee that they won't know for sure that it was us that took it."

Marcus smiled briefly. "Sounds good to me. Joey, I'm going to hang around here today, if you don't mind. I'd like to be here if those two come back."

"Sure. We'll even put you to work."

Marcus gave a thumbs-up.

Joey turned to the table. "Anyone have anything else?"

No one did.

"Okay, let's get to work. Jim, if we can help with your current cases, just let us know. Also, please see Tony. He'll give you some grunts to help any of the three of you with personal effects or clothes that you might want to bring from your homes."

"I will. I know that Lena is crying about her makeup."

"Tony will have someone take care of it. Marcus, can Misty and I talk to you in my office?"

"Sure."

Everyone stood and left the situation room, off to take care of whatever errands needed to be taken care of. Joey, Misty, and Marcus headed for Joey's office. Joey stopped at Turk's desk.

"Turk, the three of us have lots of things to discuss. I'm not saying don't disturb us, but please make sure that it's important."

"Will do, boss." Turk fidgeted. "You got a visitor."

"Who is it?"

Turk looked pointedly at Marcus. "Not sure I should say right now, boss."

"Oh, for God's sake," said Joey. "Write it on a sticky note."

Turk did, and showed it to Joey. Joey laughed.

"You can send him in, Turk."

"You sure?"

"Yeah, it's all good."

"I'll have Tony send him up."

"Thanks."

The three continued into Joey's office. Once inside, Misty couldn't wait to satisfy her curiosity.

"Okay, Mister, spill it," she said, smiling.

Joey laughed again. "Mr. Rizzo is here to visit. Turk doesn't know that a truce was called in Chicago, and he didn't know how Marcus would take the news."

"Might be good to see him again," said Marcus.

"Joey, you know if he's here, it's because Mickey Giambini sent him," said Misty.

Joey nodded. "I know. We'll find out in a minute. Marcus, we'll have to talk after Rizzo leaves. I want to throw an idea at you, and see if it sticks."

Marcus shrugged. "I'm here all day, Joey."

Soon, there was a knock at the door.

"Come in!" called Joey.

The door opened, and Rizzo walked into the office, smiling widely.

Rizzo was Mickey Giambini's right hand man. Mickey Giambini ran an organized crime family in the city. Joey had once killed a man in Giambini's private office, and Giambini had added money to the bounty that Esteban Fernandez had placed on Joey's head. But a truce between them had been established with the Chicago mission. Justice Security and the Giambini crime family weren't enemies, but they weren't friends, either. They respected each other for what they were.

Joey met Rizzo halfway into the office, and shook hands with the man. Rizzo also shook hands with Marcus, and he kissed the back of Misty's hand.

"Such a beautiful woman," said Rizzo, looking into her eyes. "If I were ten years younger, I'd give young Justice here a run for his money."

"Thank you, Rizzo," replied Misty, with blushing cheeks. She held her head high. "And what makes you think it would be a race? I'm with Joey for many reasons, and it would have to be a very, very special man to even make me consider leaving his side."

Rizzo smiled. "Can't blame a man for trying, though, Misty." He turned to Joey. "Can I speak freely in here?"

Joey read that as being *Can I talk in front of the FBI man?*

Marcus took the hint, too. "I'm going to step downstairs to the lobby and speak with Tony for a few minutes, Joey. Is that okay?"

"Thanks, Marcus. That would be great."

Marcus left the room.

Joey turned to Rizzo. "Have a seat, Rizzo. Would you like a shot of that Irish whiskey that you enjoy?"

"As early as it is, I don't think I can resist. Yes, please, if it's no trouble."

Joey shook his head. "No trouble at all, Rizzo."

Joey crossed to the bar, and poured a shot of very expensive Irish whiskey. He brought it to Rizzo, who took a sip.

"Wow. As delicious as the first time. Thanks, Joey."

"You're very welcome. Now what does Mickey want with us today?"

Rizzo took another sip, and let the liquid sit on his taste buds for a moment. "Wow. One thing that the Irish can do very well." He shook his head with pleasure. "Mickey wanted me to point out something odd that happened to us recently."

"Odd?" asked Misty. "What do you mean by 'odd'?"

"Well. Here goes." Rizzo took a deep breath. "We recently had a...disagreement with an officer over one of our poker dealers. We sent a team of four guys to track this cop down and kil...I mean, *discuss* the situation with him."

Joey looked at Rizzo over tented fingers. "And did you?"

"That's just it. The cop is still alive, but the team is gone."

"Brazil?"

Rizzo looked puzzled. "No, we had people there watching for them. They never showed up. And the thing is, Joey, we never found their car. Not a piece. Not a lug nut. Nothing. It's like the earth opened up and swallowed them."

"I hope Mickey doesn't want us to do anything to this cop." There was a matter-of-fact tone in Joey's voice.

Rizzo shook his head. "No, not at all. The cop is golden, and can live his life away where he is. Mickey wondered if you could maybe check out what happened to our four guys. We got nuthin'."

"Have you guys looked for them?"

Rizzo nodded. "We have, Joey. Not a trace."

"Is Mickey going to pay us to check it out?" asked Joey, smiling.

Rizzo smiled back. "I think he hopes you'll do it as a favor. But I think he might be persuaded to offer a small...stipend for expenses."

"Is he in a hurry?"

Rizzo shook his head. "Not at all."

"Good. We're in the middle of something right now, but we might find time to give it a look later on. Who are the missing guys?"

"Moses Turley, Gino Blasi, Joe Flore, and Guido Tolani."

Misty had taken out a pad and wrote down the names.

Joey spoke again. "And the cop's name?"

"Alan Blake."

Joey watched Misty until she finished writing. "And where did they disappear, Rizzo?"

Rizzo looked pained. "That's the rub, Joey. This place...I think Mickey's a little leery of it. He won't go near it."

Joey tilted his head. "And what about you?"

"It gives me the fuckin..." He shot a look at Misty. "I'm sorry. I mean, it gives me the creeps. There's just somethin' about it that doesn't jibe."

Joey smiled at his guest, and his apology to Misty. "You still haven't told me where they disappeared."

Rizzo looked at his glass, and suddenly drank the rest very quickly. He took a deep breath, and said, "They disappeared in Sardis County."

Joey nodded. He was surprised, but didn't show it. "It may take us a while to wrap this up, and it may take a while to poke around there, Rizzo, but tell Mickey we'll see what we can find."

Rizzo placed his glass on the coffee table, and stood. "Thank, Joey. I'll tell him."

Rizzo shook hands again with both Misty and Joey, and left the office.

MARCUS WAS SHOOTING the breeze with Tony as Rizzo came out of the elevator. Rizzo nodded at the two men, and left the building.

"Wonder what he's up to?" said Marcus.

Tony shook his head. "Not a clue, Marcus."

Marcus turned to go back upstairs, but turned back to Tony. "Tony, where is Jim?"

"He's gone to his apartment to pick up a few things. I sent Brandon to Emily's place, and Patty went to Lena's." He looked at Marcus. "Did you need him for something?"

Marcus frowned. "No, I just had a twinge. Probably nothing."

Marcus was deep in thought as he went back to the fourth floor.

JIM CAUTIOUSLY UNLOCKED the door to his apartment. He held his gun in his hand, and his hand along the side of his body, so that he didn't raise any alarm with neighbors that might be watching. He pushed the door open, saw nothing, and eased inside.

Nothing.

No one was in the apartment.

Jim closed the front door, and went into the bedroom with caution, but he could feel that no one was there.

He got his suitcase out of his closet and began packing for an extended stay at the Justice Security building. He allowed his mind to wander over the possibilities of what was happening, both in the case and in his personal life.

BRANDON KING UNLOCKED the door to Emily Owens' apartment, and walked inside. He wasn't very concerned about intruders, even though Tony had briefed him on why he was picking up Emily's belongings. *It would be pretty low down to go after a secretary just for something like this.*

Brandon looked around, then went into the bedroom to find Emily's suitcase. He didn't have a clue as to what she would wear, or would want to wear. The closet was full of matching tops and bottoms, so Brandon just chose things that didn't clash, or things that complimented each other. He carefully folded them, and put them into the suitcase. He then found a drawer that contained frilly nightgowns, and some flannel pajamas. He chose two pairs of pajamas, and two nightgowns. He then found Emily's underwear drawer, and packed all of the bras and other undergarments that were in the drawer.

When he walked into the bathroom to pack her makeup and personal care products, Brandon almost turned and ran away. The bathroom counter was packed. There wasn't a half inch of space to be found. It would take two suitcases to pack all of this stuff. *And* this *is why I begged Tony to send someone else. What the hell do I take, and what the hell do I leave?*

Bravely, Brandon chose things that looked like they had been used recently, along with a hair dryer, a curling iron, and a few other female power tools.

I hope I picked the right stuff. I don't want Emily mad at me. Hell, I don't want Turk *mad at me!*

PATTY FERGUSON SLOWLY opened the door to Lena's apartment. The apartment was dim inside, and Patty could see that the drapes weren't open. She didn't see anyone inside.

She stepped inside, and closed the door behind her.

When the door clicked shut, someone immediately linked their arms around Patty's, and clasped their hands together behind her head. She struggled for a moment, but whoever had her whirled her around to face the interior of the apartment.

As Patty came to a stop, a light came on beside an armchair. Agent Johnson sat in the chair, smiling lightly. He was dressed in the same off-the-rack suit as the day before.

"Well, well, what have we here?"

"Let me *go!*" said Patty, as she twisted a bit.

Johnson stood. "I don't think so. At least, not quite yet." He came within a foot of her. "And who might you be?" He looked at the name plate on her chest, then at the patch under the badge on the other side of the shirt. "Patty Ferguson. Justice Security." He nodded and smiled. "Interesting. Doesn't this place belong to someone from your competitor?"

Patty said nothing. She had an advantage. She knew who this man was, and she had a real good idea who held her arms behind her. She was studying Johnson. She decided to give him one last chance to let her go. "Who are you, Mister?"

"You can call me...Johnson."

Patty's eyes narrowed. It was time to show these two what she was made of. Using her right leg, she stomped on Smith's foot as hard as she could with her uniform boots. Smith grunted, and bent slightly with the pain. Patty's left arm shot out of Smith's grip, and, like a piston, drove her fist into Johnson's face as hard as she could. She then reached behind her with the same arm, grabbed Smith's coat close to the collar, and bent over quickly, throwing Smith over the top of her head, and into Johnson. Both men fell to the floor, and Patty opened the apartment door and ran. She turned a corner just as the two ment burst from the apartment, but she had too big of a head start on them, and soon lost them in the pedestrian traffic around the building.

Patty stopped running once she realized that the two men were not behind her. She leaned against a building, and bent over, trying to catch her breath. Once her breathing was under control, she flagged down a taxi, and gave the driver the address. As she rode, she called Tony on her radio.

"Patty, what happened?"

"Those two guys in the sedan from yesterday were inside Lena's apartment. They thought they had me, but I taught them otherwise."

"Are you okay?"

"I'm fine, just winded. I'm in a taxi on the way to you now."

"I'll be watching. Be careful."

"I'll be fine, Tony." Patty smiled as she put away her radio. *Shot in Chicago, and ambushed at someone else's apartment in my home city. Wow. What else can happen to me?*

As Patty rode in the taxi, she could see several blocks ahead. In the distance she could see an armored vehicle weaving in and out of traffic on the city street at a rapid pace. As it approached, she realized that it was a Justice Security armored Humvee, full of RRGs – Rapid Response Grunts. These were the Justice Security elite force, comparable to a police force SWAT team. This group had been implemented after the attack on the Justice Security building during the nightclub massacre. Patty realized that they had been mobilized after her call, and that they were heading to Lena's apartment.

They zipped past the taxi, and she watched them through the taxi's back window until she couldn't see them. Patty turned around and settled back into her seat.

Maybe the RRGs will catch those two bastards.

The taxi driver had watched her in his rearview mirror. He then noticed her two-toned brown uniform, and realized that she was from Justice Security.

"Um, Miss?"

Patty focused on the man's eyes in the mirror. "Yes?"

"Uh...nobody's going to shoot at me with you in the car, are they?"

Patty smiled and shook her head. "I sure hope not. Now, they might take a shot at *me*..." She didn't finish the sentence.

The driver sped up.

AT THE AIRPORT, LOUIE and Jessica had just climbed aboard one of the two Justice Security private jets. The pilot, an Air Force veteran named Gena Trotter, met them just inside the door.

"Welcome aboard. The closest airport to our destination is located in Tucker's Corner. They have only two landing strips, but the longest one should accommodate us easily. Our flight time should be about four hours, give or take, since we're flying into a headwind. I contacted the airport, and they'll have a rental car waiting. Helping me fly today is Pat Lambdin. The weather is clear all the way to Tucker's Corner, so our flight should be an easy one."

Louie, ducking a bit so that his head wouldn't bump the ceiling of the small jet, smiled at the pilot. "Thanks, Gena. Sounds great!"

The pilot closed the plane's door. As she entered the cockpit, she turned back and told the two, "We'll be taking off in about five minutes."

"Excellent! Thank you!" called Jessica.

Gena shut the cockpit door behind her.

Five minutes later, the plane took off.

Jessica unbuckled her seat belt after the plane had leveled off. "Louie, what do you think we'll find out from this Utley man?"

Louie smiled a scary smile. "Anything I want to know, Jess." He began flexing his hands into fists. "Anything."

THE TAXI DRIVER DROPPED Patty off in front of the entrance to the building. She got out, paid the man, and he sped off as fast as he could. Patty was still chuckling to herself as she entered the building.

There was a mob waiting for her in the lobby.

Every partner that was in the building was there, along with Tony Armstrong and Dr. Orville Eugene ("Call me Buddy") Bishop, the Justice Security staff physician. All were asking her if she was okay.

Patty actually looked a little fearful, but responded with, "I'm fine. Really."

Dr. Bishop stepped up to her, touched her chin, and tilted her face up so that he could get a good look at it. "No one hit you?"

Patty shook her head. "No. Smith just grabbed me from behind, and put me in a headlock. I got out of it, and did some damage to them before I ran out of there."

Dexter asked the next question. "What did you do to them, Patty?"

Patty took a breath. "Okay. I walked into the apartment. The blinds were all closed, so it was dark inside. I shut the door behind me, and Agent Smith grabbed me from behind, and put me in a headlock." She continued, and explained everything that happened at the apartment.

"You *go*, girl!" said Megan enthusiastically.

Dexter beamed with pride. "Those are good moves I taught you, aren't they?"

Patty smiled at him. "Yes, they are."

Dr. Bishop pronounced, "Joey, she's fine. Good as new, and unless she has a sprain or something from throwing the guy, Patty is healthy."

Joey turned to her. "I'm sorry, Patty. It may seem as if we're blowing this way out of proportion, but I don't want to lose anyone. Especially one of my new plainclothes people."

It took a few seconds for the remark to register with Patty. When it did, she laughed, clapped her hands, and did a few little jumps of excitement. "Really? Now? I'll take it!" She impulsively hugged Joey while she was jumping. "Thank you! Thank you!" She let go of him, and hugged Misty. Then she hugged Dexter, then Megan. She hugged everyone in the group.

When she was done, she stopped, and looked at Joey. "Sir...are you promoting Brandon, too? I can't accept this unless he's getting the same promotion. He's my best friend."

Joey looked steadily into Patty's eyes. "So it means that much to you?"

Patty stood straight, and returned the look. "Yes, sir. It does."

Joey looked down at the ground, shaking his head. "Patty, I hate to tell you this, but..." He looked up at her, and saw the tears welling in her eyes. "But Brandon is promoted, too. You're both ready."

Patty squealed again and started jumping up and down. Then she hugged Joey again, saying, "Thank you!" over and over.

Brandon came through the front doors then, carrying two obviously heavy suitcases from Emily's apartment. He looked around at the group gathered there, and said, "Did I miss something?"

Chapter 11

"We'll be landing in ten minutes," said Gena Trotter, over the intercom. "Time to buckle up, folks."

Louie and Jessica both buckled their seat belts.

Again, Gena's voice came over the intercom. "Local time is 11:50 AM, with the time zone differences. The car waiting for you is a dark blue Honda Civic." Gena paused. "Apparently, there aren't very many landings at that airport. We seem to be big news."

"Ain't that just great." Louie was not in a good mood.

Jessica patted her partner's hand. "Don't be grouchy, Louie. It'll all come good. You'll see."

Louie curled his lip and growled.

The private jet touched down gently, then taxied over to the hangar.

Louie and Jessica unbuckled, and gathered their belongings. Gena and Pat came out of the cockpit. Both ladies stretched as much as they could, then Pat opened the small door. The door also functioned as a stairway to the runway.

The four people stepped down and stretched. As they stretched, a short, balding, portly man walked over to them. He held his hands wide, and his smile was almost as wide as his arms.

"Welcome to Tucker's Corner! I'm Winston Alister, and I run the airport here! If there's anything I can do for you during your stay, just say so! We have a maintenance man on site, if you require maintenance on your jet, and we also have fuel. Your rental car is parked over in the parking lot, and here are the keys." He handed the keys to Jessica.

Jessica smiled as she accepted the car keys. "Thank you, sir. Anything needed for the plane should be addressed by Captain Trotter or Captain Lambdin. I would imagine that we need refueling at the very least."

"Of course, of course!" Alistair turned to Gena. "Would you like to taxi over to the fuel tank? If you'd rather not, we have a fuel truck that can refuel you on the runway."

Louie interrupted. "Gena, if ya'll need anything, call our cells. We're headin' in, so do what you need to do. We'll want to leave as soon as we're done."

"Yes, sir." Gena turned to Alistair, and began running down what she needed as Louie and Jessica moved toward the parking lot.

"For a small town, this place sure does offer good service," said Louie.

Jessica nodded. "It does."

They came to the Civic, and climbed in. Jessica was driving, Louie in the passenger seat. The car was the latest model, and had built-in GPS. Louie programmed the bank branch's address into the GPS unit. Once the unit had planned the route, Jessica began driving.

"How do you want to approach things with Mr. Utley, Louie? Besides punching and hurting, I mean."

Louie laughed. "I don't care, Jessica. You come up with a plan, and I'll follow your lead."

Jessica smiled as she drove. "Thank you. I'll come up with something fun and off the wall, I promise."

The rest of the drive was quiet, with the exception of quiet music in the background from the car's satellite radio.

"THE RAPID RESPONSE unit didn't catch them, Marcus." Joey sat down behind the conference table in the building's situation room.

"Can't say I'm surprised." Marcus closed his briefcase. He had been looking at some files sent over by the city's FBI office. "My runner just said that they had no idea who those guys were. They found two more IDs with their photos. One was NSA, and the other was Homeland Security."

Misty looked puzzled. "How can someone get IDs for all these different agencies without tripping some kind of alarm?"

Marcus shook his head. "Usually, with something like that, what we're doing right now *is* tripping the alarm. Turf wars in Washington are very real, and the different turfs are guarded jealously. You can work for more than one agency, and nobody notices, because they don't share information. Not unless they have to, anyway."

"Idiots." Joey shook his head. "That kind of crap wouldn't fly in the private sector. Hell, Jim would be dead if he hadn't come to us when he did. And not through any fault of his own, either. I'm just waiting to see if..." Joey's eyes widened, and he hastily picked up the desk phone. He dialed an internal number, and started talking. "Dexter. Have you run those two photos through the CIA system yet? Well, then, can you do it right away? Thanks. Let me know."

Marcus looked at Joey. "You really think they're CIA?"

Joey shook his head. "I doubt it. But I bet they have IDs from them."

"What did you want to talk to me about earlier?" asked Marcus.

Joey shared a look with Misty. She nodded. "We're thinking of making Jim a partner in the company."

"I don't see a problem with that, Joey. He already has clearance for government contracts." Marcus looked at both of them. "There's more to this, isn't there?"

Joey smiled lopsidedly. "Yes. We want Jim, but we want one other person as a partner, too. We want them to open a branch office for us, with Tory overseeing them."

"A branch office?" Marcus grinned broadly. "It's about time! Who's the other person you want for a partner?"

Joey told him.

"Wow! And where do you want this branch office?"

Joey told him that, too.

Marcus was incredulous. "You have *got* to be kidding! What in the *world* is *there* to warrant a branch office?"

Misty and Joey explained their thinking. Marcus stared at the two of them at first, and then gradually began to nod his head.

"Okay, I can understand that...maybe. But, good luck with that second partnership. It'll be a tough sell."

Joey smiled. "Maybe not as tough as you think. But none of this leaves this room, Marcus."

Marcus shrugged. "No problem. I can keep secrets with the best of them."

BRANDON AND PATTY CAME back from a late celebratory lunch.

After telling Brandon that he was promoted, Joey pulled both of the young people aside.

"Misty and I need to talk to you two later this afternoon. Come to my office when you get back from lunch. I have an idea to throw at both of you."

All during lunch, the two friends wondered what could possibly be the reason for calling them to his office.

"Think it's something bad?" wondered Brandon.

Patty laughed at him. "Don't be paranoid! Joey wouldn't have promoted us just for something bad!" She took a bite of her cheeseburger. After she chewed and swallowed, she said, "I bet it's something special."

Brandon agreed. "Yeah, probably. But what could it be? I haven't heard any chatter about anything going on, except this Jim Dandy thing."

Patty nodded. "I know. I wonder if it has to do with him."

Brandon munched a French fry. "Could be. But, now that I think about it, there's a lot of stuff that happens on the fourth floor that we never hear about."

Patty took a bite of one of her own French fries. "True that, Brandon. They play their cards pretty close to the vest up there."

As the two came into the front door, Tony said, "I wish I could keep banker's hours, like certain plainclothes security people."

Realizing that he was playing with them, Patty retorted, "Get promoted, Mister." She and Brandon stopped at the desk. "Tony, why haven't you ever taken a promotion to plainclothes? I'm sure it's been offered."

Tony looked at the two of them. Then he smiled. "You're right. It's been offered. Many times. Trouble is, I don't know what it feels like outside of a uniform." He shook his head. "After I got out of the service, I started working here. I just like the feel of the uniform, I guess...and no one would ever believe me if I had to go undercover." He waved them off. "Now, scram. The boss is waiting for you."

"Any idea what he wants?" asked Brandon.

"Kid, you can find out yourself in about thirty seconds! Now, beat it!" Tony shooed them away.

When the elevator opened on the fourth floor, Turk smiled when he saw them. He was blunt and short as always. "They're waitin' for you." He jerked a thumb toward the office door.

In front of Joey's office door, the young friends shared a look, and, together, took a deep breath. Patty reached out and knocked.

"Come in!" called Joey.

Brandon opened the door, and the two stepped inside.

"Come in, you two! Close the door."

Patty closed the door, and turned around. Joey, Misty, and Marcus were all sitting in the meeting area of Joey's office. Joey and Misty were on the couch, and Marcus was in one of the armchairs.

Misty gestured to the love seat. "Please sit down."

They did.

"Guys, I have an idea cooking that I'd like to share with you two. But, it has to remain in this office. Not a word outside. Am I clear?" Joey gave them each a stern look.

"Yes, sir." Brandon and Patty said it almost in unison.

"Okay, here's the deal...we've offered a partnership to Jim Dandy. We want him and one other person to open a branch office, and we want you two to head up plainclothes investigations there."

Both Patty and Brandon had wide, surprised eyes.

"WE'D LIKE TO SEE MR. Utley, please." Jessica looked down at the sitting secretary.

"I'm sorry, Mr. Utley is busy today. Do you have an appointment?"

"Oh, I'm afraid we don't." Jessica gestured at Louie. "My business partner and I have just come into some money, and we'd like the bank's advice as to the best way to invest it. We were told that Mr. Utley was the person that could best advise us." She leaned forward and whispered. "It's a bit over twenty million dollars." She stood upright and spoke normally. "But, if he's too busy to see us, I'm sure that there's another bank in Tucker's Corner that could help us." She and Louie turned to leave.

"Just a moment!" called the secretary. "He's got a cancellation in just a few minutes. Let me tell him that you're here." She stood, and walked over to an office door. She knocked, then went inside. She was inside for a few seconds, and came back out to her desk. "He'll gladly see you. Go right through that door."

Jessica gave a regal nod to the secretary. "Thank you so very much." She and Louie went over to the door and knocked.

"Please come in!" came from the other side of the door.

Jessica opened the door and walked in.

The man behind the big desk was standing, and smiling...until Louie walked in. The man looked up into Louie's face, and the smile faltered a bit. The man gulped.

Jessica said, "Luther Utley?"

"Y-y-yes, th-that's me. What can I do for you?"

Louie closed the office door, and flipped the lock. He turned around, crossed his arms, and smiled.

Utley almost wet himself.

Jessica smiled sweetly at him. "Mr. Utley, my name is Jessica Queen. I'm a partner at Justice Security. I'm sure you've heard of us?"

Utley began looking upset. "Y-yes...yes, I have."

"Oh, I'm so pleased. This rather large gentleman with me is one of my partners, Percival 'King Louie' Washington."

Utley gulped, and held out his trembling hand as if to shake.

Louie didn't move. But he did continue smiling.

"Mr. Utley, perhaps you could do us one small favor, in the interest of National Security. Perhaps you'd be willing to tell us who owns the numbered account in which you deposited Esteban Fernandez' payoff money?"

Utley's mouth moved, but no sound came from it.

"Mr. Utley, you wouldn't want to make Mr. Washington...*angry*." She looked at him with wide eyes. "Now, *would* you?"

"I-I-I d-d-don't kn-kn-know," stammered Utley.

Louie uncrossed his arms and gave Utley a stern look. "What do you *mean* you don't know?" His voice was low and menacing.

Utley held out a shaking hand in a 'stop' gesture. "I-I-I m-m-mean I-I d-d-don't kn-know! I-I'm j-j-just guh-given a n-n-number to ruh-route it to! I duh-don't kn-know the n-name! Honest!"

"Mr. Utley, surely you don't think we *believe* that, do you?" asked Jessica sweetly. "How can you not know who the money is going to?"

Utley looked at Jessica as if she was his savior. "I-I receive a special coded deposit. The code is encrypted, and I have the key. I decrypt the code, and follow the routing instructions. I ask no questions, and for this service, I receive ten percent of all monies that I pass on."

Louie took a step forward. His voice remained low and menacing. "Just what the *hell* makes you work for somebody like Esteban Fernandez?"

A dark stain showed at Utley's crotch, and spread down his leg as he urinated on himself. "Muh-muh-money, of course."

"Oh, this is terrible, Mr. Utley," said Jessica gently. "You see, we have the entire conversation with you recorded on a small, pen-sized video recorder. We'll simply *have* to phone for the FBI to come and escort you to a place away from here. I'm quite sure that they'll ask you many more questions than we have." She put both hands on his desk and leaned forward. Her voice changed, and became very stern and frightening. "*Unless* you tell us everything you know, I'll make certain that you disappear into Guantanamo prison. That's where National Security threats are placed. And with our Federal credentials, we can make sure that you have an extended visit."

Utley gulped audibly. "I swuh-swear, I've tuh-told you all I knuh-know."

Jessica looked him in the eye. "You know, Louie...I believe he has." She took out her phone. "Would you like to call them, or shall I?" Then, Jessica winked at her partner.

JIM DANDY HAD JUST settled in behind his desk in the temporary Jim Dandy Security office in the Justice Security Building.

This desk doesn't feel right. I want my big one.

He stared at the empty desktop. It had the usual desktop supplies, but it was empty of personality, as if it were waiting for its rightful owner to come along and make it shiny and special.

It doesn't make any sense to put it off any longer. Joey and Misty told me that if I wanted to do the partner thing, that I could talk to Emily and Lena anytime...but, once I do that, I have to talk to our people. Extend the invitation, so to speak. How can this be so hard?

Jim tapped out a quick drumbeat on his desk. He tried not to let the threat from the last couple of days get to him as he went about his day's affairs.

Which didn't amount to much.

And this relocation thing. I'm really not sure if Emily and Lena would be interested in it. It's such a long way from the city...although, I understand Joey's need to have another secure place to go, just in case things heat up too much here in the city, and I'm flattered that he wants me to take care of it for him. So what's really bothering me about this?

He stood up abruptly, looked around, and sat back down.

Is it the loss of identity? I mean, it would mean the end of having my name on the company door. Jim shook his head. *Am I really that vain?* He shook his head again. *Joey's bringing in money hand over fist, and I only rent the top floor of a semi-decent building. And he's inviting me to oversee the construction and staffing of a branch office. It really might be better to share the risk, and know that I've always got backup.*

Jim nodded to himself. *That trumps the whole thing right there. Even with this vendetta with Fernandez, chances are excellent that joining Justice Security as a full partner is definitely the way to go.*

He picked up the desk phone, and dialed the outer office. Emily answered. "Yes, sir?"

"Emmy, come in here. We need to talk."

LOUIE WAS ON THE PHONE with Joey, just outside Utley's office.

"Yeah, you should have seen us, man. Me and Jess work well together."

"That's great, Louie! And you say the FBI is there now?"

Utley was in handcuffs, just then being escorted out of his office, and through the bank.

"Yeah, they're takin' him in now." Louie paused. "He didn't know much, Joey. He didn't know who gets the money. All he ever knew was the account number."

"Do you think he'll make it to trial?"

Louie snorted. "Depends on how big Fernandez thinks this guy is. But, my guess would be no. Fernandez doesn't have a lot of patience with stuff like that."

"Which, again, makes me wonder why someone would risk it all that way." Louie could hear a touch of sadness in Joey's voice.

"Joey. You can feel bad for this guy all you want to. But remember this: *he chose to do it.* Nobody made him do it. He could have said no, and Fernandez' people would have found somebody else that would've. Whatever trap he's caught up in is his own fault. Period."

"I hear you, big guy. So, changing the subject, are you and Jessica going to Los Angeles to check on Charlie?"

"Yeah, unless you need us right now, we're planning to head that way."

"Nah, go ahead. If Carly isn't passed out from something, get her to autograph a picture for me. I got space on my wall."

Louie burst out laughing at his partner and friend.

AGENT JOHNSON CLOSED his phone and said to Agent Smith, "We've been ordered back to D. C."

Agent Smith grunted. "Big surprise."

Agent Johnson smiled at his partner. "But we've been given one last job to do before we go."

Chapter 12

Joey burst into Jim's private office, and was out of breath.

Jim had just finished talking with Emily and Lena, and both had agreed to go with Jim to oversee construction of the new building, and both had been delighted to join Justice Security, mainly because it meant big raises, and good benefits.

Jim looked at Joey, and saw the urgency in his eyes.

"What's wrong, Joey?"

Joey took one more deep breath. He had run down the stairs from the fourth floor. "The Sullivan building is on fire." He took another breath. "The top three floors are ashes, and word is that the entire building is about to go up."

Jim, Emily, and Lena all looked at Joey with disbelief.

"What happened?" asked Jim.

Joey was back to breathing normally. "From what I could find out, the fire department believes it was arson."

Lena's mouth dropped open, Emily burst into tears, and Jim looked stunned.

Finally, Jim said, "My *desk!* Rex Stout used it, and now it's gone! *Damn* it!" He slapped the top of his current desk. Then he looked up at Joey. "Do...do you think we should go over there, Joey?"

Joey shrugged. "We can, if any of you want to, but I don't recommend it."

"Why?" asked Lena.

Joey hesitated. "Two reasons, Lena. One, there's nothing left on the top floor...literally. Two, well...it could be a trap to lure you back there."

"Lure us back there?" asked Lena.

Joey nodded. "It would be easy for those two men to take a shot at you in the crowds, or grab one of you and haul you away...it's just best to stay here, and let the fire department do their job."

Jim nodded. "He's right, guys. This just became real for us." He looked up at Joey. "I'm in, and so are these two. Jim Dandy is a partner in Justice Security."

Joey smiled. "That's great, Jim. I'm really happy. I'll get the lawyers to draw up the papers now."

"Since I'm a partner, does that mean I can use the lobby? I need to talk to my people. I'd like you there, too, if you don't mind."

Joey nodded. "Sure. I'd be glad to."

Jim looked at Emily and Lena. "Ladies, when you've pulled yourselves together, get all of our operatives here this afternoon at five o'clock. We're having a fire sale at Jim Dandy Security."

THE LOBBY WAS CROWDED at five o'clock, but not very much.

Lena and Emily had drafted Turk and Tony to help them call everyone in. Less than five of Jim Dandy Security's operatives had not made it to the meeting...but almost one hundred people had shown up.

Tony had pulled in several former Jim Dandy employees...all of them were people that now worked for Justice Security. There was a great deal of handshaking and laughter between the former employees and the new employees.

At five o'clock on the nose, Jim Dandy spoke into the wireless microphone.

"Ladies and gentlemen, thank you for coming on such short notice." Jim looked around the room. Emily and Lena stood close to him, along with Joey, Misty, and Megan. Dexter had remained in the computer lab. "I'm sure all of you know that the Sullivan building is history." Several gasps went through the room, and some said things like 'oh, no' and 'what are we going to do now?' Most just looked blank, but some looked angry, and others looked confused. "Jim Dandy Security is no more. It's closed. Out of business." Loud cries of 'What?' and 'Why?' came through clearly. Jim held his hand up for quiet. "It isn't because of the fire. This decision had already been made when the fire started." Jim smiled his hundred-watt-smile. "I've been offered a partnership with Justice Security." Shocked silence followed this announcement. Finally, someone in the back began clapping. Another joined in. Soon, everyone was applauding.

Jim was surprised at this reaction. He held his hand up again for silence. "The great part is that each and every one of you has been invited to work with us here at Justice Security."

This time, the applause was thunderous. Every single one of Jim's current and former employees were applauding as loudly as they could.

Once more, Jim held his hand up. "So, does that mean you all want to work here?"

The applause was again thunderous, and even louder than before. Not one of Jim's people turned down the offer. They knew what those two-toned brown uniforms meant in this city, and were proud to be considered good enough to wear them.

Jim smiled his smile again, and the noise died down. "Well. Welcome to Justice Security, then."

As the tumultuous applause and whistling began to die down, Joey indicated that he wanted to speak to the group. Jim passed the microphone to him, and stepped off of the small stepladder that had been brought out for this. Joey stepped up onto it, and faced the crowd.

The cheers and applause died down as everyone saw that someone else had stepped up. When it was quiet, Joey spoke into the microphone.

"Hi. I'm Joey Justice."

More cheers and applause.

Joey raised a hand to quiet the group down. "Thanks, but you may not feel that way in a week or so."

The group laughed at the joke.

"Seriously, we have paperwork that needs to be filled out, and salaries that need to be discussed. Emily and Lena have agreed to help our HR people in that regard, and so has Tony Armstrong. Tony, wave at these guys so they'll know who you are!"

Tony, behind the front desk, waved his arm so that everyone could see him.

"For those of you in uniform, Tony will be your supervisor. He'll dispatch you to the various jobs we hold. If there's a place you'd like to work, or a part of our company that you'd rather be in, such as Building Services or Accounting, tell us, and we'll work with you to see that you get it, if at all possible. We have vacancies everywhere." Joey took a breath. "Those of you that are used to working plain clothes, we'll have you covered as well. Now, for the part you need to pay attention to." There were a few groans and loud sighs. "Sorry, guys. Every employee at Justice Security must be proficient with a firearm. You will be armed at all times. We don't accept jobs that ask for unarmed personnel, and we tell the client why – this is a dangerous job. If you are in uniform, you're a target. It doesn't matter whether you're a cop on the street, or a security job inside a grocery store. That uniform is a bullet magnet, and your survival...or the client's survival...may depend on you being able to shoot back."

Many of the people in the crowd had serious looks on their faces.

"Second, all employees here learn basic hand-to-hand moves that will help you defeat the average criminal on the street. These two things are not negotiable. If you feel that this isn't for you, the front entrance also opens out. None of us will hold any grudge against you."

No one moved to the door.

"One last thing you have to be aware of before you can sign up...Esteban Fernandez has declared war on Justice Security. He's insane, highly intelligent, and extremely dangerous. You could die the next time he comes to town. Every member of this company is to have their last will and testament on file with our law offices, and a person designated to make decisions for you in case you are no longer able to make those decisions. It's a sobering thing to think about, but it's a necessary one."

Joey smiled grimly. "So...if all of that is acceptable to you, welcome to Justice Security!"

Loud applause and cheering again ran through the lobby.

Jim had taken back the microphone.

"Okay, Lena and Emily are over beside the cafeteria, along with some people from Human Resources. Line up, and let's get this rolling!"

All of Jim's people began having conversations among themselves as they lined up.

Not one single person at the meeting had chosen to leave.

Megan was impressed, and said so. "Jim, you have a really loyal group of people here. I'm very impressed with that."

Jim's smile was ear-to-ear. "I'm proud of them, too, Megan. Joey, I think you've inherited a great group of people."

Joey looked at Jim. "Jim. *We* have inherited these people. You're part of us now, and we'll always have your back."

Misty nodded. "And we're so glad to have your friendship again."

Jim nodded. "I'm glad to be with you guys, too."

"Okay, could we please stop being so sugary? It's making me dizzy." Megan placed her hands on either side of her head.

The others laughed.

"CALLING KCPX, THIS is JS-001, entering your airspace, over."

"This is Carson City, JS-001. We have you on radar, over."

"Thank you, Carson City. This is Captain Trotter. We are en route to LAX, and we request any air traffic in the area, please. Over."

"Roger that, Captain Trotter. We show you to be flying at twenty thousand feet, at one hundred fifty knots. You are just fine on the path you're on, Captain. The only other radar chirp is a bug in the area. It fades in and out. Over."

"Acknowledged, KCPX. We show the same radar pattern. It's mostly showing up behind us, over."

"Roger, JS-001. We believe that it isn't anyth..."

The words were drowned out in the Justice Security cockpit. A stealth fighter passed less than fifty feet over them, then banked to the east. The backwash rocked the small jet violently

"KCPX, KCPX, this is JS-001! We have just been buzzed by a stealth fighter! Repeat, we have just been buzzed by a stealth fighter! Do you know of any military flights in this area? Over!"

"Negative, JS-001. We'll get on the horn and make some calls, over."

"The fighter banked to the east, Carson City. It's out of sight right now. Radar ghosts behind us are gone, too. Over."

"Roger that, JS-001. We suspect that was the source of the blips. But we're showing them a mile behind you and coming up fast. Over."

Just then, a blip appeared on the small jet's radar. Gena noticed it. *Oh, shit.*

"Pat, get on the intercom phone. Tell Louie and Jessica to sit down and put on their seat belts, and tell them why. Now!" She then began speaking with the tower again. "Carson City, I have them on my radar screen as well. Are there any other aircraft in the area? I need some room to maneuver. Over."

"Negative, Captain Trotter. You're all clear to do what you need to do. The Air Force assures me that none of their planes are in the air. We will attempt to contact the plane. Stay on this frequency. Over."

The plane had just begun flying over the Mojave Desert. To Gena's starboard, or right side, she could see the Sierra Nevada Mountains. Below, she could see only desert.

Pat hung up the phone and told Gena, "Louie said, quote, 'Tell Gena to keep my ebony ass in one piece.'"

Gena smiled as she concentrated on flying the plane.

The Carson City tower came back on the air.

"KCPX calling JS-001, do you read? Over."

"Loud and clear, KCPX. Over."

"Bad news, Captain. The stealth fighter does not answer." The speaker paused. "We haven't got a clue who it is. Over."

A small contrail passed by the plane. The contrail was following a small missile.

Gena's eyes widened. "KCPX, KCPX! This is JS-001! The fighter has just fired a small missile at us! Repeat, the fighter has just fired a small missile at us! It missed, but not by much! Over!"

"Dear God, Captain, bring that plane lower! Now!"

Gena pushed the stick forward, and the plane began to lose altitude. The intercom phone rang, and Pat answered it. The color drained from her face as she listened to what Louie told her. Still holding the phone, she turned to Gena.

"Louie says that a number of holes have appeared in the roof and the floor back there. He says they're bullet holes."

"JESSICA! SOME MOTHERFUCKER is *shooting* at us!" Louie was strapped into his seat, and glared at the bullet holes that had appeared six inches in front of his feet.

Jessica snapped back at Louie, as she stared at a line of bullet holes in the fuselage wall beside her. "*Thank* you for sharing the bleeding obvious!"

"KCPX, KCPX, WE ARE being fire upon! Over!"

"Roger that, Captain Trotter. Can you begin some evasive maneuvers? Over."

"Never occurred to me, KCPX!" snapped Gena as she began banking the plane back and forth. "Carson City, I show that we're about a hundred miles from you. I want to declare an emergency, and need immediate clearance to land! Over!"

"Already done, Captain. Runway Ten is clear, and emergency equipment is standing by. Over."

"Acknowledged, KCPX. Thank you. Over."

Pat suddenly shouted, "Port engine is on fire, Captain!"

"*Who the fuck is shooting at us?*" screamed Gena, both at Pat and to the Carson City tower. "KCPX, we are going down, repeat we are going down. We are going to try an emergency landing in the desert. Our port engine is on fire, and we have almost full fuel tanks. Please have emergency equipment come to us as soon as possible, and notify Justice Security that we have been shot down. Over."

"Roger, Captain. We show that you're about seventy five miles from us. Be careful. The desert may look level, but there are lots of bumps. Contact us when you've landed. May God be with you. Over."

Gena was fighting with the stick. The port engine had lost most of its power, and it was all she could do to be able to hold the plane steady.

"Okay, no landing gear. We're going in belly first, Pat."

"Okay, Gena."

They were at five hundred feet, then four hundred. Smoke poured from the port engine, and occasional flames could be seen peeking out.

Gena flipped the intercom on so that she could speak through the microphone in front of her mouth. "Louie, Jessica, brace yourselves. It's going to be a rough landing. I'm sorry. I've been shot at, but never been shot down before." She began to level out the plane. They were now fifty feet above the desert. From what Gena could see, it looked level enough. Occasional cactus plants could be seen, but it was mostly dirt, sand, and small rocks.

"Here we go, Pat. Help me keep the nose up as much as I can."

The plane dropped slowly, with the nose slightly up. Air speed had dropped to twenty five knots, and she couldn't risk it any slower until they were on the ground, because the starboard engine might stall, and the plane wouldn't have any power at all.

The back third of the plane kissed the ground, and brought the nose down abruptly. It started sliding across the desert floor.

"Pat! Power off the port engine! Dump the fuel! Now!"

Pat complied with the order by pressing a couple of buttons.

"Fuel dumped, Captain!"

The plane was still sliding at twenty miles an hour.

"Powering down starboard engine!"

The plane slid past a three-foot-high boulder. The port wing was just low enough to be snapped off as they passed it. The jolt shook the plane all the way through.

"Port wing is gone, Captain!"

The plane was still sliding. Both pilots were so focused on their gauges and equipment, that they didn't see the pile of boulders directly in front of the plane. The nose hit them head-on at seventeen miles an hour, and stopped abruptly. The nose of the plane had been crumpled from the impact. Behind it stretched a half-mile-long rut in the desert.

The stealth fighter passed over the plane once, then banked toward its home base.

No sound came from the plane, except the occasional creak or pop from the metal as it expanded slightly in the intense heat. The dust stirred up by the plane's rough landing began to slowly settle back to the ground.

A desert iguana peeked out from beneath the rocks, gradually inched a small distance at a time until it had climbed to the top of the rocks, and, once there, it began warming itself in the desert sunshine.

Chapter 13

Mark Haase was minding the phones and the front desk as Tony assisted with enrolling the new employees. The lobby was noisy, which made hearing any phone calls difficult.

"Justice Security, this is Mark Haase. May I help you?"

"Mr. Haase, you don't know me. My name is Cole Nelson. I guess I need to speak to someone in charge."

"Mr. Nelson, all of the main partners are either out of town, or busy at the moment. Perhaps if I knew the nature of your call, I'd know how to get you to the right person. I don't need details, just the general nature of the problem."

"Mr. Haase, I work the tower at the Carson City, Nevada airport. Somebody in a stealth fighter just shot down one of your planes."

Mark knew that the only plane Justice Security had in the air was on the west coast, carrying Louie and Jessica. He found that he couldn't speak.

"Mr. Haase, are you still there?"

Finally, Mark was able to make a sentence. "Sh-shot down?"

"That's what it looked like to us."

"C-ca-can you hold on for a moment? I'll get the partners that are on site to the phone immediately."

"I sure can, Mr. Haase."

"Thanks, Mr. Nelson." Mark put the phone on hold, and then pressed the button that connected him to the intercom system that ran throughout the building.

"May I have your attention, please? I need everyone's attention."

The room quieted down, and Mark continued.

"I need all partners on site at the front desk immediately. It's an emergency."

Joey, Misty, and Megan walked briskly to the desk. Marcus joined them. Misty turned back to look at Jim.

"Come on, Jim, you signed the papers. You're a partner now."

"Oh, yeah, I forgot. I'm sorry." Jim walked quickly to stand beside his new partners.

"What's wrong, Mark?"

"Sir, I think you'd better wait for Dexter. Then you can all find out together. It will save time."

Tony wandered over, and so did Turk. Turk was holding hands with Emily.

The stairwell door opened and shut, and Dexter ran to the front desk.

"What's going on?"

Mark took a breath. "There's a phone call that you all need to hear." He picked up the phone receiver, and accessed the intercom again. "Would everyone in the lobby please remain silent? We have an important phone call that the partners need to have on speakerphone. Thank you." Mark then pressed the button for the phone call from Nelson, and put it on speakerphone. "Mr. Nelson, are you still there?"

"I'm right here, Mr. Haase."

"You're on speakerphone, sir. I have with me Joey Justice, and several of the partners of Justice Security, and they're all standing here with me. Would you please repeat what you told me?"

They could hear Nelson take a deep breath. "I'm Cole Nelson. I run the tower for the Carson City, Nevada airport. According to radio reports, and from our own radar, it appears that a stealth fighter has shot down one of your planes."

The ladies all gasped, and Dexter had to hold on to the desk to stay upright. Megan put her arm around him, and put her head on his shoulder.

Joey spoke. "Mr. Nelson, this is Joey Justice. Do you have any details?"

"Well...to be honest, Mr. Justice, I'm not really sure that I'm supposed to say anything until the incident has been investigated."

Marcus spoke up. "Mr. Nelson, my name is Marcus Moore. I'm the Section Chief for the FBI office in this city. Justice Security handles many top secret contracts for the United States Government. I authorize you to give any details to Mr. Justice that you have available. I'll give you a few moments to look up the phone number for the FBI office, and verify what I've told you, and that I'm here in the Justice Security Building."

Nelson paused. "Mr. Moore, I'm going to do just that. I'm putting this call on hold while I call." There was a click, then the line hummed.

Joey whirled on Marcus. He didn't yell, but he spoke forcefully. "You put your people to work right now on this. Find out who had a stealth fighter up, and why. Somebody powerful is behind this, Marcus, and I'm through messing around with it. And if Louie, or Jessica, or either of the two pilots are dead from this, I'm gonna fuck somebody's day up *really* bad. And, if I have to, I'll get Mickey Giambini to help me."

"I'll put them right on it, Joey, and some people in Washington, too. I know a few people in CIA and NSA. I'll find out something. You have my word."

The speakerphone came back to life. "Mr. Moore, I spoke with your secretary. She told me that to verify your identity, I should ask you this: Who's your best friend?"

Marcus spoke almost before Nelson finished. "Nicholas Turner."

"Then I guess it's you, sir." Nelson paused. "Our radar was picking up a ghost signal...kind of a 'blip', if you know what I mean."

Joey nodded and said, "We do."

"It faded in and out, like most stealth technology. Nothing you could get a lock on. At first, it was just following your plane. Then, it buzzed it. Your Captain Trotter was quite upset throughout the situation, but she kept her head, and kept right on flying. The stealth fighter fired a missile at her, but it missed. Then, as closely as I can figure, the fighter opened fire on her, and a bullet took out her port engine. The last thing I heard from her was that she was going to perform an emergency landing in the desert. She dropped below our radar, and we never had another transmission from her."

Misty spoke up. "Mr. Nelson, this is Misty Wilhite. Were there any survivors?"

Nelson sighed. "Honestly, Ms. Wilhite, I just don't know. We've dispatched a helicopter with paramedics to their last know position, but, until they find the crash, we won't know anything."

"Sir, my name is Dexter Beck. Is there anything we can do here? Or can we help if we come to you?"

"Mr. Beck, I'd welcome all the help I can get."

Dexter turned to Joey. "Joey..."

Joey held up a hand. "Hold on, Dex. Mr. Nelson, is there anything else you can tell us right now? Were you able to see which direction the stealth fighter took?"

"No, I'm sorry, Mr. Justice. I was too busy keeping up with your plane, and on getting the emergency people responding to the crash. I didn't pay any more attention to that thing. And, right now, I'm sorry to say that I don't have any more information for you. Not until they find the crash site." Nelson paused. "I wish I knew more. I'm sorry."

Joey shook his head as he answered. "Not your fault, Mr. Nelson. Thank you for all you've done. We'll be in touch, because I'll definitely be sending some people to you."

"I'll be waiting, sir." Nelson disconnected the call.

Joey's mind was still trying to wrap itself around the fact that someone had shot down one of their planes, and that Louie and Jessica could be hurt...or dead. Not to mention Gena and Pat. His thoughts whirled, then he nodded once to himself, as if to say that he'd make up his mind.

"Dexter, can you spare Megan?"

Dexter looked puzzled. "Sure, Joey, but I want to go."

"I know you do, Dex. We all want to. But I can't spare both you and Megan. I need one of you to keep digging at that account number, and I need my best person. No offense intended to Megan, but you're the one, Dexter."

"It's fine, honey," said Megan. "Joey's right. You're needed here more than ever. You're our best chance at finding out who, or maybe where, they are. And, if I know my partner Joey, we're going to fuck some people up. Am I right, Joey?"

"You're damn straight, girl!"

"I need a phone," said Marcus. "Can I use the situation room, Joey?"

"You don't even have to ask, Marcus. Of course you can. Megan, when you go, take Patti and Brandon with you. Use the other jet. Marcus, do you think you can arrange some military assistance under our contract? Can you check into that? I'd like for the plane to be escorted. Mark, I need Tony here. Will you go with them?"

"Of course I will!"

"Good! Next, we'll..."

"Excuse me, sir," interrupted a voice behind Joey. Joey whirled around. It was one of the Jim Dandy people.

"Mr. Justice, my name is Harvey Paxton." The man waved his arm around the lobby. "Sir, if there is anything any of us can do, we stand ready to back your play, right down to the ground, if we have to." Paxton stood ramrod straight, all six feet of him, arms at his sides, betraying his military background.

Everyone in the lobby cheered and applauded loudly following Paxton's words.

Paxton spoke over the din. "We're proud to work for you, sir, and it seems like someone has hurt one of our people. We want some payback, sir!"

Joey was overwhelmed by the outpouring of loyalty from all of the people gathered there. He waved his arms for silence, and waited for them to quiet down.

"Thank you all. We'll have our payback, and when I find who did this, we'll all get a piece of them. I promise you, they're goin' *down!*"

The applause actually vibrated the glass in a couple of places in the lobby.

MAMA! YOU GOT TOO MUCH wood in that stove again! It's burnin' up in this house!

Louie moved his head slightly.

Ow! That hurt! Who the hell pounded on my head? They done a number this time, feels like.

He moved his head again, this time from the left side to the right. His head swam, and he felt nauseous.

Hell *no, I ain't throwin' up! Bastard'll see that I'm hurtin'! Who the hell did it? Pyle?*

Louie shook his head, and the pounding inside made sure that he wouldn't do it again.

Naw, it couldn't be Pyle! I beat that sumbitch! Knocked him clean out with one good punch. See? I can hear him moanin' now!

"Ohhh," came the moan.

Pyle sure does sound like a woman! Wonder if he's a fairy?

"Louie," came a voice. "Louie, are you alive? Can you move?"

Louie opened his eyes wide. One of them, anyway. The other felt like it had a red cover on it.

Standing over him was Jessica. She held her left arm at an odd angle, and her face was puffy and bleeding. She was tapping his cheek with her right hand.

"Jessica! What the...!" Louie tried to move, but his head swam like it was going down a drain. "Oh, God, what happened?"

"A piece of the dining table hit your head pretty hard when we crashed. You bled a lot, and I think you might have a concussion."

Louie was still belted in to his seat, and it all came back to him. Getting shot down, seeing the engine on fire, the belly landing, the wing snapping off, and that final abrupt halt.

"Oh, shit, Jess, you mean we alive?"

"We're alive. My left arm is broken, and my face is going to look like I just got out of a bar brawl, but we're alive."

He reached down and unbuckled his seat belt. It seemed as if it took an eternity to do it, but he got it, and collapsed back into his seat after he had undone the belt.

"How 'bout Gena? Or Pat? You checked on them yet?"

"Pat's dead, Louie. Gena is alive, but she's pinned in her seat. We hit some boulders...that's why we stopped so quickly. Pat was crushed by her stick, and Gena is pinned by hers. I was waiting for you to wake up, because I can't move her with only one arm."

Louie was struggling to make his mind focus. "Does she have anything broken? Like a rib, or her neck?"

Jessica shook her head. "No, she's got some small cuts and some bruises. That's all."

Louie put a hand on each side of his head, and leaned forward toward his knees. "Jessie, baby, it might take me a minute."

Jessica nodded. "Okay, Louie. I just need to sit down for a..."

She never finished the sentence. Louie looked up just as Jessica's eyes rolled up into her head, and her knees buckled. She fell to the debris-scattered floor. Louie tried to catch her, but his head swam so badly that he missed his grip. The dizziness took over, and Louie collapsed to the floor of the plane, too.

Both of them swam in and out of consciousness, in the desert heat, on the floor of a crushed and ruined plane.

MARCUS WAS SPEAKING sternly into the phone when Joey, Misty, and Jim entered the situation room.

"I don't care who you wake up, or who you disturb. You find out who authorized a stealth fighter to shoot down an unarmed private jet. Use whatever you have to, but I want a name, dammit!" He slammed the receiver down on the desk phone.

"No luck, Marcus?" asked Misty.

"Not yet. But I'll find out. You can count on it."

A look of determination was on Joey's face. "You can bet that I'm going to find out. God help whoever ordered this, because I'll want them sent to Guantanamo, Marcus."

Marcus nodded. "Interfering with an investigation with possible National Security repercussions is strong enough for that to happen." Marcus' voice was calm, but he was furious inside. "Oh, before I called my people, I arranged for military escort for Megan's flight. Their orders are to shoot down even Air Force One if it come near that plane." He smiled. "Well, not really Air Force One...but you get my drift."

Joey nodded. "I do. I wish Nelson would call with some information. I'm really worried right now."

Jim looked up. "I'm sorry, Joey."

Joey looked surprised. "Sorry for what, Jim?"

"I'm sorry for getting you into this. I feel responsible."

"Jim, you didn't do this! They were hitting every security company in the city! It could have been anybody!"

Jim nodded. "Yeah, it could have. But it wasn't. It was mine. And I pulled you into it."

Joey leaned forward. "Jim. You are our friend, and now our partner. We signed papers to that effect this afternoon, and you own one-seventh of the stock of Justice Security, Incorporated." He pointed his finger at Jim Dandy. "When one partner is in trouble, we *all* come running. That's how we built this company, and that's how it's always going to be. Nobody is at fault here, and we'll get the bastard behind this, or die trying."

Jim nodded. "That's the part I'm afraid of, Joey. If anyone dies, it's my fault for bringing it down on them."

Misty shook her head. "It isn't, Jim. We've contracted to bring down Fernandez...we would have run into this at some point, anyway. Better now than later."

Marcus agreed. "And, besides, if you hadn't come to Joey, you'd be dead by now, Jim. And so would Emily and Lena. The only fault here is on the person or persons that are trying to hide the fact that they're accepting payoffs from Fernandez. That's who we'll bring the world down on top of if someone dies."

"KCPX TOWER, THIS IS Rescue One, over."

"Go ahead, Rescue One. Over."

"We've spotted the plane, KCPX. It's in the desert about fifty miles east of your location. Over."

"Roger that, Rescue One. Do you see any sign of survivors? Over."

Rescue One was a large helicopter with medical equipment and paramedics on board...basically, a flying ambulance. The pilot keyed his microphone, and said, "Negative, KCPX tower, but we haven't landed yet. It looks banged up, and it's missing the port wing, but it's mostly intact. Survivors may be inside. Over."

"We have you on radar, Rescue One. Please advise after you've landed. Over."

"Roger that, KCPX tower. Over."

The pilot banked the chopper just enough to correct his flight path so that he could land the helicopter as close to the plane's door as possible.

LOUIE COULD HEAR AND feel the pounding of the helicopter blades. He struggled to stay conscious, and forced himself to sit up. He looked at Jessica through his clean eye, and saw that she was still unconscious. He slowly leaned over and grasped her under her arms. He then pulled her to him, and placed her head in his lap. He closed his eye, and let his head swim for another moment.

He could tell by the sound of the blades that the chopper had landed beside the plane, and someone was pounding on the door, trying to open it.

Louie gently brushed hair from Jessica's face, and tapped her cheeks lightly. "Wake up, Jessica. We're saved, baby, we're saved."

Jessica's eyes fluttered, and her Australian heritage appeared. "Bloody well better be, mate!"

Louie began chuckling. Jessica, realizing what she had said, chuckled along with him.

The pounding on the plane door had stopped. The rescuers had gotten the door open, and were coming inside.

"Hi. I'm Evan Anderson. I'm a paramedic. I'm here to help you. How many of you are there?"

Louie looked up with his clear eye and said, "Four. Us two, and the two pilots. One of the pilots is pinned by the stick, man, and I couldn't stop bein' dizzy long enough to get to her. Jessica here said that the co-pilot is dead. Said she was crushed by the stick when we hit the rocks."

"I see. Well, let me see to your friend here, and these other guys will go see about getting your pilot loose." Anderson reached for Jessica.

Louie put a hand on Anderson's arm. "Careful, man. Her arm's broken."

"He's not a bloody idiot, Louie. He can probably see that for himself." Jessica's voice was testy.

Both men chuckled.

They could hear men in the cockpit, and they could hear Gena's voice as the men got her free.

The lone female paramedic called out. "Hey! We have a pulse on this one! Let's try to get her out of here!"

The paramedic that was checking Jessica's vitals said, "Looks like your dead pilot is alive after all."

"Oh, thank the good Lord," said Louie.

TONY'S VOICE CAME OVER the radio.

"J-1, do you copy?"

Joey grabbed his radio. "Go ahead, front desk."

"Cole Nelson on line 2, boss."

"Thanks, Tony!"

Joey answered the phone call on speakerphone.

"Mr. Nelson! This is Joey Justice. What can you tell me?"

"Mr. Justice, initial reports from Rescue One say that all four people that were on the plane are alive. They're banged up pretty bad, and the co-pilot is in critical condition with several fractured ribs, but they're all alive."

Chapter 14

J ustice Security's staff physician, Dr. Orville Eugene (Call me 'Buddy') Bishop also left with the group going to Carson City. His explanation to Joey was brief and to the point.

"They're our people. I'll make certain that good care is taken, or I'll break the Hippocratic Oath and hurt some people."

Dexter had called Megan as soon as Joey had spread the word about the crash victims.

"Honey, tell Louie that I said it would take more than shooting down a plane to take him out."

Megan smiled. "I will, sweet love. We're taking off, so I need to go. I love you."

"I love you, too, Megan," replied Dexter.

When the private jet took off, it was escorted by two F-16 fighter planes.

THE FBI CELL PHONE that Marcus always carried rang. He excused himself from the conference table in the situation room, and stepped away to answer it.

Misty stole a look at Joey. She could sense that he was growing angrier and more frightened by the minute. She shared that anxiety for her fiancé, because she felt it, too. She leaned toward him, put her hand on his, and squeezed it gently.

"Joey," she said quietly. "It will be okay. Louie and Jessica will be fine, and so will Gena. Pat will get some great care, and be back flying in no time. Megan and Dr. Bishop will see to that."

Joey covered Misty's hand with his. "I know, love. But, it makes me angry that this is happening at all. It's not Fernandez for once, but someone that he's paying off. Everything lately keeps coming back to him."

"Then we'll just have to take steps to eliminate the problem."

"But, Misty, don't you see? If it isn't Fernandez, it would be someone else. Drug money is so easy to make, and payoffs are so easy to take just so someone will look the other way. How do you stop that?"

Misty smiled slightly. "Joey, you know the answer to that. We can't stop all that's wrong in the world. We're just one company that caught the attention of a Mexican drug cartel leader by accident. It could easily have been Jim."

"But it wasn't Jim, Misty. It was us, and we did it with a la-la-la attitude. People have died because of this feud, and it all could have been avoided. We weren't grown-up enough to recognize the forces we were playing with."

Jim leaned forward in his chair. "Joey, you forget that I was there with you when you first met Fernandez. Remember the explosives in the arena? You didn't set those. None of us did. Fernandez set them, and he did it with the intention of scaring the residents of our city into compliance with his wishes. We stopped that bomb, you and I. You and Misty stopped him at the nightclub. You guys stopped him in Chicago. His luck is going to run out, Joey, and when it does, Justice Security will be there to make his world turn really painful." He leaned back in his chair again. "Listen to Misty, you big dumbass! She's trying to make you understand that we'll beat this, too."

Joey shook his head. "Yeah, maybe so, Jim. But what will be the cost? I've almost lost two friends today. I don't want to lose any, if I can help it."

"Joey, we all know the price we might pay, every single time we step out of this building," said Misty. "The only thing we can do is train ourselves, and be prepared. We have to think on our feet, and use what's at hand. Most of all, we have to survive...but if we can't, the best we can do is make our sacrifice mean something." She leaned close to Joey. "If Louie, or Jessica, or Gena, or Pat, or anyone else in this company had died trying to stop whoever is behind this, it would have been for a good reason. It would have meant something. If we bring down just one...just *one*...bad guy, it's worth it, because it means we've made the world a little bit better." She smiled into his eyes. "To quote Mickey Giambini, *capisce?*"

Joey smiled back at Misty and nodded. "*Capisce.*"

Marcus turned to the three partners. "We've been summoned."

The three looked up at Marcus, and Joey said, "What?"

Marcus repeated his statement. "We've been summoned."

"Summoned where, Marcus? And who summoned us?" asked Misty.

"Jim, you weren't here when the contract was signed, so you won't know about this. Joey, Misty, do you remember that one of the requirements for your Fernandez contract was to testify to certain Congressional Intelligence committees?"

Joey nodded. "I do. So what?"

"Senator Howard Thompson, the chairman of the Senate Intelligence Committee, has summoned all on-site partners and their liaison, me, to report to Washington immediately."

Joey slumped down into his seat. "Now?"

"Well," said Marcus. "Not immediately. In the morning."

"Great," said Misty. "We don't have a plane. One plane is dead, and the other is taking Megan and the others to help the crash victims."

Joey shook his head. "The stealth choppers won't make it that far. I guess we could take one of the cargo planes if we have to."

"The senator's office said that they would have a plane at the airport for us at 7:30 in the morning," said Marcus. "They gave me the gate number, plane number, and the necessary things to do to get past security quickly."

"Well, as far as the senator is concerned, Dexter is out of the office. I really need him here, so that he can keep working on finding the owner of that numbered account." Joey looked determined. "So, that leaves me, Misty, and Jim. We're it."

Marcus shrugged. "I don't know anything about Dexter's whereabouts. The senator will have three partners there, so that should be good enough." He looked at Jim. "When Joey and the other signed the government's contract to bring down Fernandez, one codicil was that Justice Security would have to testify occasionally to various committees."

Jim nodded. "I understand. But, I do have a question about this sudden summons." He folded his hands together on the table in front of him. "Why now?"

Joey looked curiously at his old friend and new partner. "You know, I hadn't thought about that." He turned to Marcus. "He's right. Why now? I mean, Chicago was weeks ago, and we haven't had any progress on Fernandez lately. Why now?"

Again, Marcus shrugged. "I don't have a clue, Joe. I guess we'll find out tomorrow."

THE FLIGHT CREW OF the second private jet was made up of a pilot and a co-pilot. The pilot was Captain David Crews. His co-pilot was Billy Baker. Both had only been working for Justice Security for less than a year, so they were all business with Megan as she climbed aboard. Nothing she did seemed to put the two of them at ease.

Of course it could have something to do with fear of being shot down.

With this thought, Megan turned to Patty Ferguson, who sat in the seat beside her.

"Patty, do you think the pilots are afraid we'll be shot down, too?"

Patty, who was terrified of flying, answered, "If they are, they aren't alone." Her hands gripped the armrests on her seat so tightly that her knuckles had all turned white.

Brandon and Mark sat across from them, facing the back of the plane. The ladies faced forward. The fixed table was between the two sets of seats. Dr. Bishop had settled into one of the bunks in the sleeping area, and snored lightly as the plane flew toward Carson City, Nevada.

"Patty, I don't know if it helps, but if we get shot down, we probably won't even know it." Brandon smirked as he joked with his best friend.

Patty gave Brandon a look that would melt steel, and a universally recognized, one-finger salute.

Mark smiled to himself.

Megan noticed Mark's smile, and said, "What's funny, Mark? These two?"

Mark nodded. "Well, yeah, but that's not why I'm smiling. This is the first field job I've been on in some time. I haven't been assigned outside the building since the night that Donna shot me."

Megan winced. "Oh. That." She thought for a moment. "Have I ever mentioned how lucky you and Jessica were that night?"

Mark smiled at her. "A couple of times."

"Fernandez shot me," said Patty through gritted teeth. "In Chicago. If I hadn't had my vest on, I would be dead right now."

"I was shot by a ricochet inside the helicopter when we first tried to take out Fernandez." Megan shuddered. "It isn't fun, is it?"

Both Patty and Mark shook their heads.

Brandon said, "I guess I've been lucky. Nobody's shot me yet."

Patty retorted, "Smartass. Be glad I'm too scared to get my gun out right now. Your leg would be toast."

Megan and Mark laughed at the two young people.

Mark peeked through the window beside his seat. "Well, I guess we're still being escorted. I can see one of the fighters out there."

Brandon was concerned. "Where did the stealth fighter come from? The one that shot down our plane?"

Megan shook her head. "We don't know yet, Brandon. We *do* know that it was someone with the authority to order a black operation. It had to be. You can't just fly a stealth fighter over the country without somebody giving an order okaying it."

Patty considered this. "So, if that's the case, it has to be someone within our government."

Megan nodded. "That's what we're thinking."

Mark looked out the window at the F-16 flying with them. "Great. Now they don't look like protection. Now they look more like threats."

JOEY AND JIM TOOK MARCUS to the computer lab. Misty had gone upstairs to the apartment she shared with Joey. She told Joey that she would join them later.

"How's it going, Dexter?" asked Joey.

"It's pissing me off, that's how!" Dexter's fingers flew across the keyboard. When they stopped, he pointed to a moving yellow line on the screen. "See that? Every time I try to trace that account, somebody tries to trace back to me, and I haven't found a way around it yet. But I will." His fingers flew across the keyboard again. "Of course, it doesn't help that I'm worried about Louie and Jessica, and Megan, and the pilots, and everybody else. I can't concentrate as hard as I normally concentrate." He stole a glance at the two of them. "No word yet, I suppose?"

Jim shook his head. "No, nothing yet."

Dexter's attention was on the yellow line again, which had disappeared for a moment, but had now reappeared. "*Damn* it!" His fingers flew across the keyboard again, and the line disappeared.

"Do you even know the bank yet?" asked Marcus.

Without looking up, Dexter answered. "No. It's in Switzerland, but that's all I know so far."

The three men watched Dexter for a while longer.

Joey spoke. "Dex, we're going to the situation room to wait for word from you, or word about them."

"That's cool, Joey. *Damn* it!"

IN THE CARSON CITY hospital, Louie had insisted on being in the room with Jessica as the doctors checked her out. He refused treatment for himself until she had been taken care of. At first, the two doctors had said that it wasn't permitted, but a glare and a few choice words from Louie convinced them otherwise.

Jessica's arm had been broken when her seat had come loose from the floor, and smacked into the seat facing her. Her hand had been out to try to deflect the impact. The doctor said that it was a clean break, so that setting it would be simple. Jessica insisted on holding Louie's hand while the arm was set. She only cried out once, but Louie's hand felt as if it had been squeezed in a vise.

The cut on Louie's head required seven stitches. He also had a concussion, and the doctors were adamant about him spending the night in the hospital, no matter how many fierce glares he gave them. He agreed, but only if he and Jessica shared a room.

"Ain't nobody hurtin' this lady while I'm here, and that's that," Louie told them.

So, he and Jessica were to spend the night in the hospital.

Gena had a small cut on her forehead that required three stitches. Her ribs had been bruised, but not broken. She could leave whenever she chose, according to the doctors, but Louie overrode that.

"She stays here until Dr. Bishop gets here. If he says go, she can go."

So, Gena was waiting, seated with Louie and Jessica in their shared room.

Pat didn't fare quite as well. She was in surgery, and it didn't look good. Her ribs had been fractured. Both lungs had been pierced, and one rib had nicked her heart. She was bleeding internally, but the hospital staff was doing the best it could.

Unfortunately, it wasn't enough. Pat Lambdin passed away quietly while undergoing surgery.

When the head surgeon entered the room, all three of them knew right away that Pat didn't make it.

Gena began crying quietly.

Jessica said, "Oh, bollocks!"

Louie cursed loudly and thoroughly.

Joey was going to be ten kinds of pissed off. *And when he's pissed off, there's no stoppin' him. God help whoever did this, 'cause if Joey don't get 'em, I sure will!*

The door to the room opened, and Megan walked in. She was talking on her phone, and she looked around until her eyes landed on Louie.

"I'm looking at him right now, honey," Megan said into the phone. "No, he doesn't look any better...just more banged up." She strode to Louie and hugged him fiercely. Louie hugged her back.

Louie had tears welled up in his eyes when the hug stopped.

"No, he looks fine, Dexter. He just has some stitches in his empty head." She listened for a moment as she hugged Gena tightly, then walked to Jessica's bedside. "Jessie has her arm in a cast, and she looks like Louie took her into the ring for a sparring match." She hugged Jessica gently. "Yes, Dexter, Gena's fine. She has some stitches on her forehead, but it's a tossup between her and Louie as to who is more banged up."

The door opened again, and Patty, Brandon, and Mark came into the room. They each hugged the survivors as Megan talked to Dexter.

"No, Dr. Bishop is still talking with the chief surgeon here at the hospital about Pat. From what we were told, she was hanging on borrowed time as it was. Dr. Bishop seems to think that the people here did their best." She listened. "No, she just slipped away while they were operating. Her ribs were basically smashed into shards by the stick, and were floating around inside her, punching holes wherever they landed. Her lungs were pierced, and there was a hole in her heart. Dr. Bishop will have to give details, Dex, that's all I know." She listened. "Tell Joey that I'll get the doc to call him shortly. I think he wants to check out our other people first." She listened, looked at Louie, and rolled her eyes. "Okay, sweetie, you're our only hope, then. Lose the trace, and tell them to be careful. If anyone calls from Congress, you're here with us, but you're in the bathroom. Gotcha. I love you, too, Dexter. Yes. I'll call you when we get rooms for the night. Bye!" She disconnected, then looked at the three survivors. "We got here as fast as we could. I'm so sorry about Pat."

Louie looked up at Megan. "Hey, what was that about Congress?"

Megan looked distracted as she felt Jessica's cast. "Joey, Misty, Jim, and Marcus were called to testify for the Senate Intelligence Committee tomorrow morning. Senator Thompson arranged a plane for them. Dexter was supposed to go, too, but they lied and said that he came out here with us. He's still trying to lose that other hacker that keeps chasing him away from that account number."

"Does he know where it is?" asked Jessica. Her voice was a bit slurred from the pain medication that the doctor had prescribed.

"Only that it's in Switzerland. They keep trying to trace him back every time he goes looking for that number. He needs time to figure out how to circumvent that other hacker." Megan turned to Gena, and bent over to get a close look at the cut on her forehead. "Officially, Turk and Tony will be in charge. But, with Dex in the building, he's really the one calling the shots." She focused on Gena's eyes. "Your stitches look great, Gena. Black is very becoming."

Gena smiled for the first time in several hours.

Megan stood up and looked at Louie. "Joey's royally pissed off. He's been worried sick about all of you, and Dexter said that Pat's death hit him really hard. Dexter said to tell you that Joey's face looks like it did when Vincent Lambosa killed Jennie Lou Gwin."

Louie shook his head slowly. "Oh, great. That means Joey's gonna make sure this ends bloody, don't it?" Then he shrugged. "So what? The motherfucker has it coming. Might as well step up and own it all, 'cause Joey gonna make sure this guy pays the damn bill!"

Louie looked around the room for a moment. "Megan."

"Yes, Louie?"

He jerked a thumb at Patty and Brandon. "Why the hell did you bring these two brats? I mean, I know why you brought Mark...but *these* two?"

Brandon stood to his full height. "I'll have you know, *Mis*-ter Washington, that we are a couple of the best damned plainclothes security people you'll ever find."

Patty held up a large bag of potato chips. "And we brought snacks."

Louie smiled widely. "Now *that's* what I'm talkin' about."

Chapter 15

Joey's group arrived at the city's airport at seven the next morning. Marcus had somehow eliminated the need for TSA screening procedures.

"Beats me," he told Joey. "I just did what the directions from the senator said to do."

No one was patted down, but it didn't matter anyway. No one was armed.

Marcus explained, and the others agreed. "Look, we're heading for D.C., right? We won't be allowed to have weapons inside the Capitol Building anyway, so why bring them to begin with?"

So, the group passed through to the private hangar housing the plane.

The plane was fancy. It was a 1979 Mitsubishi Mirage twin-propeller plane. The door was located just under the wing, and had a small step to assist getting into the aircraft. All four of them climbed aboard the plane, and took seats in the posh interior.

"Welcome aboard!" called out one of the two pilots in the front of the plane. "There's coffee in the galley in the rear, if anyone wants any! We're finishing out checklist now, and we'll take off as soon as we have clearance."

"Thank you!" called Misty.

The group could only see the pilots' backs, as they were already seated. Each wore white shirts with appropriate uniforms, and the usual pilot hats. Neither one looked back as Marcus, the last one on the plane, closed and secured the door at the request of the pilot.

Jim said, "Coffee for me. Anyone else?"

Everyone wanted a cup, and said so as Jim moved to the galley in the back of the plane. He had to make two trips to carry the four cups. Everyone settled in and fastened their seat belts.

The last thing they had heard from their people in Nevada was that everyone was settled in for a good night's sleep. Barring anything unusual, they would head back home as soon as Dr. Bishop pronounced them safe for travel.

Jessica's arm had been set nicely, and the cast she would have to wear for six weeks was done properly. Louie did indeed have a concussion, but it wasn't severe. Gena's bruises would heal gradually, too.

Megan, Mark, Patty, and Brandon had agreed to a round-the-clock watch on the three crash victims, just to make sure that no one came after them a second time.

The FAA had locked down the crash site. Unofficially, the Aviation person in charge of the investigation remarked that the plane had definitely been shot down, noting bullet holes through the fuselage. He also mentioned that the bullets had barely missed the seat in which Louie had been sitting, and had missed Jessica by scant inches. He said that it had taken a great deal of expertise by Captain Trotter to keep the bird in the air, and bringing it in for a reasonable landing, given the circumstances. Had the plane missed the boulders in the desert during the plane's emergency landing, the investigator's opinion was that everyone inside would have walked away from the crash with only very minor injuries.

That didn't ease Joey's feeling of responsibility, however.

Louie had been right. Joey was pissed, and he felt responsible for the entire situation that they all found themselves in. In his head, he knew that he had nothing to do with any of it, and that he was only reacting to things that had been directed to the people that he worked with. But, in his heart, Joey carried the weight of the world, and his heart placed the responsibility squarely on his shoulders.

Jim Dandy was feeling much the same way. Even though good things had come from this situation, and he was now sitting with his old college friends, holding a ticket for a D. C. plane, the fact that some of them had almost died from information that he had brought to the group weighed heavily on his mind. It soured the reunion for him just a tiny bit.

Misty Wilhite sat quietly, worried about Joey. He was taking on too much, and wouldn't talk much about what he was thinking...although, she knew full well that he was worried sick about Louie and the others. She was glad that Jim had been welcomed back into their friendship circle, but she was a bit concerned, too. She hoped that Joey didn't still harbor some jealousy toward Jim. She and Joey were engaged, after all, and that should tell him everything that he needed to know. Men could be stubborn sometimes, and read things into situations that weren't really there. She hoped that this wasn't one of those times. The situation that they found themselves in didn't bother her that much. They'd find the person being paid off by Fernandez, and they'd deal with that person. Either Marcus would arrest them, or Joey would kill them...or, at least, hurt them badly.

Marcus was thinking that, hopefully, there wouldn't be any turbulence on this flight. He really didn't want to be throwing up just before testifying to Congress. *Matter of fact, testifying to Congress is enough to make me want to throw up anyway.* His stomach gurgled, rolling the coffee around it, trying to decide if it wanted to keep it there.

The plane's intercom system came on, and a voice announced, "Hello, all! This is the Captain, and we'll be taking off in three minutes. Fasten your seatbelts and settle in, because it looks like clear sailing all the way to D. C."

DEXTER BECK HAD SLEPT for about an hour during the early morning hours. His plan was to keep working on cracking the account before Joey landed in D. C. That way, Joey could give Senator Thompson something to chew on.

One of his IT team asked if she could help him with it at all.

Dexter shook his head. "No, but thank you. I've got to figure a way around this thing!"

The lady shook her head. "It's a shame that you don't have an account there. You could waltz right in using that account, and hit them from the inside." She left to go to her cubicle to begin her day.

Dexter froze. The thought struck him hard. Could it be that simple? Just open an account with the bank that he thought had the number he was looking for, and, once in, hit them from inside. Hell, he and Megan had enough money that he could open an account with *all* of the banks in Switzerland!

With new determination, he typed in "Swiss banks" into his search engine, and began opening new numbered online accounts.

THE SQUEEZING OF THE blood pressure cuff woke Louie for what seemed like the hundredth time. He opened his eyes and looked at the cute nurse that was taking his blood pressure.

"Baby, if you weren't so cute, I'd be really mad at gettin' woke up again."

The nurse, whose name tag read "Stella", smiled at Louie as she wrote down his vital signs. "Sorry, Mr. Washington, but it's standard procedure with a concussion."

Louie smiled at Stella. "I know, Stella. But I could really use some sleep."

Jessica, in the other bed, said, "So could I, Stella. Every time you wake him up, you wake me up, too."

Gena, who was sleeping in a fold-out cot graciously provided by the hospital, said, "That makes three of us."

Mark Haase stood by the room's open door, laughing at the exchange. Louie gave Mark a look.

"What's so funny over there, Mark?"

"You three. I've never heard so much complaining. You'd think somebody shot you down in an airplane or something."

Louie started to fire back a scathing retort, but when he opened his mouth to say it, he found that he was laughing instead.

Jessica joined in, and after a moment, so did Gena.

Stella looked at the patients, shook her head, and left the room.

When the laughing began to die down, Louie said, "Ladies, are you two thinkin' what I'm thinkin'?"

Jessica said, "Probably. You want to go home, don't you?"

"Oh, yeah."

Jessica chuckled. "So do I, big guy. How about you, Gena?"

"I'd like to go home, too. When that plane started down, I thought I'd never see my daughter again. Now I just want to call her home from college and hug her until she complains about not being able to breathe."

"You hear all that, Mark?" asked Louie.

Mark was already pulling out his phone. "I'm waking them up now, Louie. I'm calling Megan first."

Louie sat up in his bed quickly. "No! Call Dr. Bishop first! I don't want Megan coming down here and going all mother hen on me!"

Mark laughed. "Okay, Louie, you got it." He stepped out into the hall to tell Dr. Bishop that there were two partners ordering them all home.

THE CHARTERED PLANE carrying Joey and the others took off at seven twenty-eight AM, two minutes earlier than scheduled.

Marcus sat erect in his chair, facing the forward section of the plane. Jim sat beside him. Joey and Misty sat across from them, facing the rear of the plane, and firmly holding hands.

Marcus had made sure that he had plenty of airsickness bags all around him. Flying normally didn't bother him...unless there was lots of turbulence, and then, he was apt to see things that he'd eaten three days earlier again.

Of course, almost every flight that Marcus had taken had turbulence at some point.

Marcus and flying did not mix well together.

His stomach growled in anticipation.

He kept his hand firmly on an airsickness bag.

Jim, on the other hand, loved to fly. It seemed to stimulate his mind and amped his muscles a bit. As a result, after every flight, Jim had plenty of energy to do what he needed to do.

Joey and Misty both took flying as a necessary part of their jobs, and didn't mind it one way or another.

But they did always hold hands tightly during takeoffs and landings. Just in case.

The plane leveled out, and clouds could be seen outside the windows.

The intercom clicked on. Jim just happened to be looking at the two pilots as the captain made his announcement.

"Okay, folks, this is your captain speaking. We're cruising at fourteen thousand feet. We should reach our destination within an hour or so."

The intercom clicked off.

Jim's thoughts ran through his mind quickly. *We're two hours flight time from D. C. How can we reach our destination in an hour or so? Did the captain make a mistake?*

Jim could see the profiles of both men in the cockpit as they turned to each other and shared a smile.

Jim's stomach dropped, and his blood turned to ice. He realized why the captain had said that they'd reach their "destination" within an hour or so.

The pilots were Agent Smith and Agent Johnson.

"Marcus!" hissed Jim quietly.

Marcus turned to Jim. His face was pale. "What is it, Jim?"

"Look at the pilots!"

Marcus looked at the two pilots. All he could see was the back of their heads.

"What about them, Jim?"

"Remember those two guys with the IDs from everywhere? They're flying the plane!"

Marcus looked again, just as Johnson glanced at his partner.

"Oh, shit. Now I'm *really* gonna throw up."

Jim leaned forward, and hissed again. "Joey!"

Joey leaned forward, and so did Misty. Joey said, "What's up?"

"The two pilots. They're Smith and Johnson."

Joey's eyes widened in surprise.

"Jim, are you kidding?"

Jim shook his head. "No. Take a look for yourself."

Misty had already unfastened her seat belt, and turned enough to peek through the seats. Joey followed suit.

Smith politely turned to whisper something to Johnson.

Joey and Misty turned back around.

"What are we going to do?" whispered Misty.

"Do any of us know how to fly?" asked Joey.

Marcus shook his head. "When it comes to flying, all I know is how to throw up."

Jim said, "I've taken a couple of lessons, but I kept getting vertigo when I was in the cockpit. I gave up on it. It seems you can't fly a plane if the height makes you too dizzy to focus."

Joey waved a thumb between Misty and himself. "Neither one of us can fly."

Jim smiled. "This doesn't look like a job for Jim Dandy."

Misty smiled, too. "Nope. No Jim Dandy to the rescue this time."

"Okay, let me pretend to go to the head, and I'll look around in the galley for something we can use to help us," said Joey.

He stood up and headed for the galley.

Behind him, he could hear Marcus throwing up into an airsickness bag.

DR. BISHOP WAS CONCERNED, and showed it.

"Are you all sure about this?" he asked his three patients.

They were all in two Carson City taxis, heading for the airport. Dr. Bishop was riding with his three patients.

Jessica answered his question. "For the umpteenth time, Doctor, we all agree that we'll heal more quickly at home."

"Yeah," agreed Louie. "We're the patients, and you said yourself that we were able to function without the hospital around us."

"We're fine, and we're sure, Doctor," said Gena.

"Well. I can't argue against it, since I'd rather have you in the building with us. And a good doctor knows when to finally shut up."

Jessica began giggling. Soon, Louie joined her, then Gena. Finally, Dr. Bishop began laughing too.

They were still chuckling when the plane took off, and the F-16 fighters took their escort positions behind them.

Gena had been greeted with solemn salutes from both David Crews and Billy Baker. She shared their Air Force backgrounds, but returned their salutes with hugs. Then the three fliers bowed their heads and said quiet prayers for their fellow pilot, Pat Lambdin.

Megan took the seat beside the telephone, used for private communication with the pilots, or for air-to-ground communication. Dr. Bishop ordered Louie and Jessica to the sleeping room, and made sure that they were securely in their bunks. He remained in the room with them should they need anything during the flight.

Patty and Brandon followed Mark Haase on board. As they had left the hotel in Carson City, Brandon had risked a dollar in a one-armed bandit that was located in the lobby.

Patty had been impatient. "Brandon, why are you wasting your money?"

The first indicator stopped spinning. The picture said, "Jackpot."

Patty continued. "I don't know anyone that's ever come out ahead on one of these things, especially one like this that's all by itself in a shabby hotel lobby."

The second picture clicked into place. It, too, said, "Jackpot."

Patty was now pulling at Brandon's shirt sleeve. "Come *on*, Brandon! We've got to *go!*"

The third picture clicked into place. It also read, "Jackpot."

Buzzers went off around the machine, lights began flashing, and a recorded voice started crowing, "Jackpot winner! Jackpot winner!"

Brandon began dancing around the lobby, and the hotel manager came out with a huge smile on her face.

"I've been here for a year and a half, and that machine has *never* triggered a jackpot win! Congratulations, sir!" She held her hand out, indicating that Brandon was to come to the front desk. "If you'll come with me, sir, I'll get a bit of information from you, and give you a check for your winnings."

Brandon, smiling ear-to-ear, said, "How much is the jackpot?"

The manager replied, "One hundred thousand dollars."

Patty could only stare at her friend with her mouth open.

Brandon waved to her, indicating that she needed to join him. To the manager, he said, "We *both* won the jackpot, and Patty and I will be splitting it evenly."

The manager smiled broadly. "Certainly, sir." She turned to Patty. "Ma'am? If you'll come with us, please?"

Mark had witnessed all of this, along with Megan, and couldn't wait to spread the story to the others.

Patty and Brandon, delighted at their chance fortune, sat back in their seats on the plane, and enjoyed the comfortable feeling that comes with a financial cushion.

DEXTER HAD FOUND THE bank.

Hertz Suisse, a small bank located in Zurich, was the bank that held the questionable account.

Dexter had figured this out by simply comparing his account numbers with the account in question. The two account number had only three digits difference.

Dexter was in the system. Cracking the password for the account was now only a matter of time, as he utilized software that he and Megan had designed specifically to break passwords.

He smiled to himself.

Now, it was only a matter of time, and he'd know the recipient of the payoffs from Fernandez. And, from the look of things, it wouldn't take long.

TONY ARMSTRONG HAD disagreed with Joey early that morning.

"Boss, you need to take some kind of weapons. With all of this going on, you'll be naked the entire time you're in Washington."

"Tony, we'll be fine. We'll have Marcus, and Marcus can call up the rest of the FBI if he has to, along with the D. C. police, the Pentagon, Homeland Security, and the Secret Service. We'll be fine."

"I still think it's a mistake, Boss."

Tony was adamant, and had stood with arms folded across his chest.

Joey sighed. "Tony, we'd only lose them at the first checkpoint going into the Capitol building. We might as well leave them here."

Tony grumbled, but stopped arguing.

But he still worried about the four of them as he sat behind the front desk.

The phone rang with an incoming call.

"Justice Security, this is Tony Armstrong. How may I direct your call?"

"This is Buck Valiant, with Champion Aviation."

"And what can I help you with, Mr. Valiant?"

"The airport cops just found my two pilots for your flight to D. C. dead in a dumpster behind the airport restaurant. But the flight took off on time. Do you know anything about it?"

Tony's stomach did a few sudden flips.

"Mr. Valiant, have you looked at the surveillance videos?"

"No, sir, I haven't. I probably could, if you want to send somebody down to check 'em out with me."

"Sir, this is urgent. May I have a number to call you back?"

"Sure." He gave Tony the number.

"I'll call you back in just a few minutes. Thanks, Mr. Valiant."

"Hey, you're welcome. I'm worried about my plane and your passengers."

"So am I, sir."

Tony disconnected the call, then called upstairs to Turk.

"Turk Wendell."

"Turk, this is Tony. Meet me in the computer lab right away. We need to talk to Dexter *now*!"

JOEY OPENED EVERY STORAGE door in the galley, and found nothing that would help them.

Finally, just beside the head, he found the emergency locker. He opened it.

Inside were two knapsacks. Both had labels on the top that read "Paradise Skydiving Club".

Parachutes!

Joey couldn't believe it! But there were four of them, and only two parachutes. That's great for two people, but what about the other two?

Also, inside the locker, Joey found two other things that he might be able to use somehow. One was an emergency life raft. The other he held for a couple of minutes, fiddled with it, then tucked it into his pants pocket.

An idea had taken root in his mind, and was beginning to grow into a plan. *It should work, and would get us all out of this mess.*

In the meantime, he filled another styrofoam cup with coffee. As he poured, he heard a voice behind him.

"J-Joey?" said Misty.

Coffee cup in hand, Joey turned around.

Agent Johnson was holding a revolver against Misty's head. He was smiling widely.

Jim and Marcus were staring daggers at Johnson, but they couldn't do anything as long as Johnson held the gun aimed at Misty.

Joey slowly walked toward the man.

"Hello, Johnson," Joey said casually.

The smile faltered a little. "You don't sound surprised to see me."

Now it was Joey's turn to smile. He pretended to take a small sip from the cup, and then said, "Made you right after takeoff. If you wanted it to be a surprise, you should have pulled the cockpit curtain closed."

A look of anger passed over Johnson's face. Then a look of determination appeared.

With his empty hand, Johnson pointed at the aircraft door. "Open that."

Joey looked at the door, and then back at Johnson. "Why?"

Johnson smiled. "Because we're going to have a little...accident. You four are going to fall a very long way, and eliminate some big problems for our boss."

"Interesting." Joey pretended to take another sip from the cup. "So, since we're all going to have a little...accident...you won't mind telling us who your boss is, will you?"

Johnson smiled and shrugged. "I don't see why not. We do whatever needs to be done for our boss, especially when it comes to keeping his name clean...like now. We work for..."

"*Senator Howard Thompson!*" shouted Dexter, just as Turk and Tony arrived in the computer lab. "*That's who the dirty son of a bitch is!*" Dexter began doing a fast boogaloo around his desk, laughing and hooting. He saw Tony and Turk, and danced over to them. He grabbed Tony, and whirled him around. "Senator Thompson is dirty, a dirty, dirty, little boy, Tony! And I got the proof! It's enough to make sure he's not re-elected *ever!*"

"Dexter, we gotta talk," said Tony, with urgency.

"Sure, sure, Tony, what's so urgent?"

Tony explained about the phone call from Buck Valiant, and what the airport police had found.

"Oh, shit," said Dexter, wide-eyed. He picked up his phone and dialed the number Valiant had given to Tony.

"Champion Aviation. This is Valiant."

"Mr. Valiant, my name is Dexter Beck. I'm one of the partners for Justice Security. My man Tony tells me that your pilots are dead. Is that correct?"

"Mr. Beck, I'm sorry to say that it is. But what bothers me is that the plane took off as scheduled, with your people aboard. Can any of them fly a plane?"

Dexter felt his stomach sinking. "No, sir, they can't."

"Then that means two men took the place of my pilots. You don't think it was damn terrorists, do you?"

"No, Mr. Valiant. At least, not the kind you're thinking of. Have you had a chance to review any security footage?"

"Not yet, but they want me to. I *do* have a digital recording of one of the pilots asking for clearance, though."

"Would you play that over the phone for me, please?"

"Be glad to. Give me just...here we go."

The recording was very clear, and very easy to understand, even over the phone.

"Tower, this is CMP fiver two niner, requesting clearance on Runway ten."

A slight pause, then: "CMP fiver two niner, you are cleared to take off on Runway ten. Fly safe."

"Roger that, Tower, and thank you."

Silence, then Valiant came back on the phone. "Could you hear that okay, Mr. Beck?"

"I know that voice, Mr. Valiant. I've heard it before, and I have photos of the two men that probably killed your pilots. Do you have any airport police there with you? Or TSA? Or maybe Homeland Security?"

"I can get them here, or I can go to them. What do you need?"

"Mr. Valiant, I need your cell phone number. I will send you photos of these two men, and you will need to review the airport security footage, and see if they can be spotted. Unfortunately, until the plane lands, there isn't much else that we *can* do."

Tony was thinking to himself again. *Boss, you should have listened to me. You're stuck in the lion's cage without a whip.*

Chapter 16

Joey was thinking fast.

"So, you work for Senator Thompson, huh? Why does he want us dead?" asked Joey.

"Truth?" said Johnson.

Joey nodded.

"All he really wanted dead was Dandy, there." Johnson waved his hand in Jim's direction. "But, you three are a bonus. If that idiot in the stealth fighter had followed the senator's instructions correctly, two more of you would be dead. But, the wiring that controlled the missiles shorted out, and the pilot had to resort to his onboard guns." He shrugged. "That's what happens when contracts are awarded to the lowest bidder, and the maintenance budget is cut."

Joey looked at Misty, hoping that they were on the same wavelength. She nodded so slightly that Joey barely saw it. But he did see it, so that meant she was ready for whatever play he was going to make.

Joey looked Johnson in the eye, measuring the twenty inches between them. "You're threatening my fiancé. You know I'm going to kill you for that."

Johnson smiled widely. "That will be quite a trick, Justice."

Joey threw the coffee into Johnson's eyes. The hot liquid burned the man badly, and he ducked down. The hand holding the gun moved away from Misty's head, and she didn't hesitate. She chopped down on Johnson's wrist with the edge of her hand, and his wrist snapped. She grabbed his broken wrist, and used her leverage to throw him over the seat, and onto the floor of the plane, directly in front of Joey. The landing knocked the breath out of Johnson. He never took another.

Joey quickly knelt down and twisted Johnson's head until his neck snapped with an audible "CRACK". It happened so quickly that Johnson's surprised look remained on his face, even after death.

"How'd you like my trick, Johnson? Good enough for you?" Joey picked up the revolver, stood, and motioned for the other three to lean in close. "Here's what I found, and here's my plan," he said quietly.

"MR. BECK, WE SPOTTED those two men on surveillance video. Turns out that they showed some kind of badges and IDs, and passed right through security. Video caught them talking to the two pilots, but there aren't any cameras covering the dumpster. But, they were definitely here," said Buck Valiant.

Dexter closed his eyes and shook his head. "Mr. Valiant, can you transfer me to either the Homeland Security agent or the FBI agent on duty there?"

"I sure can, Mr. Beck. And you're sure that these are the guys that stole my plane?"

"Yes, sir, I believe they are. And our people inside the plane are sitting ducks right now."

MARCUS WAS VERY INTENSE with his response to Joey's plan. He kept his voice down, but it seemed as if he were shouting.

"That has got to be the most insane idea that you've ever come up with! I will *not* jump out of this plane!"

Joey patiently explained it again. "Marcus, none of us can land this plane. Hell, Jim's only had a couple of lessons. None of us can fly, either. We can't sneak up on Smith and take him out because of that. If we hold a gun to his head, what's he going to do? I know what *I* would do. I would aim this plane at the ground and step on the gas, because I would have nothing to lose. That's what this guy will do if we try that. No, the object of this is to survive, and, by God, that's what we're going to do. So, we'll hook you up in one of the parachutes. You jump with Misty. It will be a little heavy, but not bad. Jim and I will jump with the second parachute. We may land a little fast, but if we roll with the landing, we should be okay. If we stay up here, we'll be dead for sure."

"I don't understand why we've got to leave this perfectly good airplane."

"Marcus, we're going. That's that."

Marcus groaned and turned even paler. "When are you planning this charade?"

Joey smiled a lopsided smile. "Now, before Smith figures out what's happening."

"Ohhhh, God!" moaned Marcus.

Looking around, Marcus realized the inevitability of the parachute jump. Shaking his head in resignation, he quickly strapped on the skydiving club's parachute.

Joey looked Marcus over, and nodded his approval. "Okay, let's get this show started." He and Misty pulled Johnson's body upright, and Misty held it as upright as she could. Joey looked at her, stepped back a bit, and shouted, "Okay, okay! We'll open the door! Just don't hurt her!"

Marcus moved over to the door in preparation, and Misty stood beside him. The plan was that he and Misty would jump as soon as he got the door open, and Joey would continue to prop up Johnson for as long as he could, or until Jim strapped on the other parachute. Then he and Jim would jump.

But they hadn't taken into account the slipstream from travelling at two hundred knots.

When Marcus opened the plane's door, the slipstream grabbed the door and pulled it open with a tremendous force, and slammed it against the side of the plane with a loud "*WHUMP*". Marcus was pulled out of the plane, but lost his grip on the door. He found himself in freefall.

When the plane door made the loud noise, Smith jerked his head around. When his head came around, his hand jerked the rudder to the side, and tilted the plane toward the open door. Misty lost her balance, and fell out of the plane.

Smith pulled out a revolver of his own, and snapped off a shot toward the back of the plane, but only managed to hit Johnson. Johnson, of course, didn't complain, since he was already dead.

Joey looked at Jim, nodded, and yelled "Go!" as Jim jumped out of the plane after Misty. Jim was holding the parachute. Smith fired another shot, and Joey returned it. He hit the man in the arm. He pushed Johnson out of the way, dropped the gun, and grabbed the two things he had set aside that he had thought might help them. Once they were in hand, he jumped out of the plane.

One of the things that he had found was a flare gun. In midair, he twisted, aimed as carefully as he could, and fired the flare gun at the plane.

His aim was lucky. The flare went in through the open door of the plane and exploded into flame. A few seconds after that, the plane itself exploded.

He looked around for his friends, hoping that Jim could catch up to Misty in time to save her. *God, if you're listening, please help my friends. Please keep Misty safe, whatever happens to me.*

MARCUS FOUGHT EVERY instinct in his body that was telling him to open the parachute.

He was falling backward, turned toward the sky. He had seen Misty fall out of the plane with no chute, saw Jim dive out seconds later and start strapping on the second parachute, and then saw Joey's dive out and fire the flare at the plane.

Marcus smiled to himself as the plane exploded. *At least Joey blew that one up on purpose, instead of an accident. Now, let's worry about getting all of us down safely.*

He almost allowed despair to get to him as he realized that two of his friends were free-falling.

How in the hell are we going to pull this off?

OH, CRAP, WHAT HAVE I done now?

Misty's surprise came as she fell out of the door of the plane.

Okay, I don't believe this.

Misty was also facing up. She saw Jim dive out of the plane while he was strapping on a parachute.

Where's Joey?

Jim wouldn't have jumped unless Joey told him to. This flew through her mind in nanoseconds.

She also knew that Jim was supposed to save her...but where was Marcus?

Misty looked around as landmarks on the ground began growing larger. She spotted Marcus. He was less than a hundred yards from her. She waved at him. He waved back.

Justice Security had its own sign language. The partners had come up with it, and taught it to most of its employees. Joey and Misty had also taught it to Marcus.

Marcus was signaling to her, since the wind whipping through their ears would overpower any shouting they could do. He signaled to her that she should angle toward him, and that when she got close and he had a hold on her, he would pull the cord and deploy the parachute.

Misty turned toward him. She angled her body slightly, with her feet above her head, and put her arms at her sides. This sped up her descent, but also allowed her to aim herself slightly by turning her legs to the left or to the right.

Oh, Marcus, I hope this works!

It did. Partially.

She reached Marcus, and they grasped hands. Misty used both of her hands to hold on to him. Marcus smiled at her and pulled the cord, deploying the parachute. The wind caught it, and abruptly pulled Marcus up.

But it also caused the two of them to lose their grip on each other.

Misty was still free-falling.

Now Jim was her only chance.

JOEY HAD BEEN WATCHING the attempt to catch Misty. Marcus actually had her hand in his, but the force of the parachute had snatched her right out of grip.

"*DAMN IT!*" he screamed at the heavens. His eyes had glossed over with tears, but whether it was from frustration and fear, or the wind whipping his face, Joey couldn't tell you.

Through the watery veil in his eyes, he could see Marcus below and to his left. Joey angled his body to attempt to intercept Marcus. At least Joey could hitch a ride with the FBI man.

The second item that Joey had brought from the plane had a rope firmly threaded through several loops on top, but loosely. The ropes expanded with the larger the item got. Joey hooked his left arm through one of the loops of nylon rope, and then put his left hand into his jeans pocket. He hoped it would hold when he pulled the release on what he hoped would be his salvation.

JOEY TRUSTED ME TO save her, and that's exactly what I'm going to do. And, if I can't, I'll die with her. Hold on, Misty, don't count Jim Dandy out yet!

Jim could see that Misty had spread her arms and legs out in an effort to increase drag on her fall, so that she would have some wind resistance, and wouldn't fall quite as fast. But, Jim knew that if he didn't reach her in time, all the drag in the world wasn't going to stop them from becoming so much hamburger at the end of the drop.

He had positioned himself in the same way Misty had when she aimed for Marcus, with his arms at his sides, his feet trailing the air behind and above him, guiding him like rudders. He estimated that he was falling much faster than she was, and that he would intercept her in seconds.

He was ten feet away from her when he called her name at the top of his lungs. The ground was coming up fast, and they had one chance. Misty was able to grab Jim, wrap both arms around his neck and both legs locked around his waist. Jim pulled the cord, and the parachute billowed out behind them. Suddenly, they were no longer falling to their deaths. They were floating down, and the wind had died down enough for Jim to hear Misty crying beside his ear.

He tilted his head to hers. It was the best hug he could give her at the moment, since he needed both hands to guide the ropes to the parachute.

"You're safe now, Misty. I have you. We're all right," soothed Jim.

"I know," she replied through her tears. "But Joey jumped without a parachute, Jim! Can we save him, too?"

To that, Jim didn't have an answer. Not one that Misty would like, anyway.

WHEN JOEY WAS ABOUT a hundred feet above and slightly to the right of Marcus, he prepared himself.

Okay, I got one shot at this. It worked in that movie, so maybe it will work enough for me to catch Marcus.

The item Joey had taken from the plane along with the flare gun was an emergency inflatable raft...the kind with its own supply of air. Joey judged the distance, and pulled the handle that automatically inflated the raft. His right arm was looped through the rope along the top as he pulled the handle, so that when it inflated, the upside down raft became a temporary hang glider. The pull on his arms was tremendously painful, but it did slow him down considerably. By pulling down with his arms, Joey was able to coast closer to Marcus. He had to take considerable pains to make sure that he didn't impact the parachute itself, but he needed to glide in underneath the billowing fabric.

Once he had done it, he yelled at Marcus much like Jim had yelled to Misty.

"Incoming!" Joey shouted to prepare Marcus.

Startled, Marcus looked up, first with fear, and then with surprise as Joey maneuvered the raft just enough to let him reach Marcus.

Marcus let go of the parachutes ropes and grabbed Joey's legs. He wrapped his arms tightly around them, and when Joey was sure that Marcus had him, he pulled his left arm out of his pocket. In his left hand was a knife with a four-inch blade. Joey slashed the raft so that it would deflate quickly, and then pushed it away from the two of them, and let it drop. He slid down the FBI man until they were face-to-face. He kept a firm grip on Marcus as they floated downward.

"Oh, God, I thought we'd lost you, Joey!" said Marcus. "Dear God in Heaven, I never want to cut it that close again!"

"Old friend, thank you for being my life preserver," replied Joey.

They were both proud of themselves for not making any jokes about "dropping in".

THE GROUND WAS COMING up fast under them.

"Okay, Misty, here it comes! Remember, let go of me when we land, bend your knees, and roll with the landing. And say a little prayer of thanks that its solid ground, and that there aren't any trees!" said Jim.

"Okay, Jim, I'm ready." Misty had unhooked one arm from around Jim's neck, and was watching their descent, trying to time the jump and roll properly.

Suddenly, the ground was there. They landed faster than recommended by skydiving experts, but they both dropped and rolled, and stood up, unhurt. The parachute billowed to the ground, and Jim unhooked himself from it. Once the chute was free, Jim collapsed onto the ground, and rolled over onto his back.

"I *never* want to do that again!" he shouted.

But Misty was watching Marcus and Joey.

Their landing wasn't quite as effortless.

"HERE IT IS, MARCUS! Remember, drop and roll, just like if you're on fire!"

With that reminder, Joey pushed away from Marcus, landed with his knees bent, and rolled away safely.

Marcus was thrown by the sudden change in weight, and landed with only one knee bent. The other was still as straight as he could hold it, and it snapped audibly when it came in contact with the ground.

"OW! *FUCK!*" shouted the FBI man when the pain hit.

Joey ran to Marcus quickly, and unfastened the parachute. It fluttered away with the wind, quickly pursuing the one released by Jim. Marcus had his hand on his leg, and he was wincing with pain.

"Lie still, Marcus! Don't move!" ordered Joey.

Misty and Jim were running to them, quickly covering the quarter-mile between the two landing points.

"I wasn't planning to. Joey, I'm gettin' too old for this shit!"

Joey smiled. "No, you're not, Marcus. You have a long way to go yet. You're just breaking in the tread."

Joey stood as Misty ran to him. She leaped, and clung to Joey much as she had clung to Jim when he caught her in midair.

"Oh, Joey, I was so scared! Not just for me, but for both of us!"

Joey held her tight against himself. "I know, Misty...I know, my love! I was, too!"

Jim knelt beside Marcus. "Broken?"

"Oh, yeah."

Jim had no idea where they were, He took out his cell phone, and called Justice Security.

Chapter 17

Senator Howard Thompson sat back in his hand-tooled leather chair and put his feet up on the massive oak desk in his Senate office.

As the chairman of the Senate Intelligence Committee, he enjoyed the perks that came with his appointment to that position by his peers...and they were many. He took advantage of several of them, too. His choice of young female interns, for instance. He liked them around eighteen and impressed with his power. If it took money to get what he wanted from them, all he had to do was assign some earmarked intelligence money, and he usually could do whatever he wanted to them. The fact that most of these girls were much younger than his youngest daughter didn't bother him in the slightest...his penis was happy with the arrangement. And, if some of the young ladies left the rendezvous with sore spots and wet tears, saying that money wasn't enough to keep them quiet, well...there were other perks that could be used to silence them. He didn't have to use those perks often, but use them he did. Anything to keep his own ass covered.

The fact that using these "perks of office" might be considered abuse of power, or even criminal acts, by the taxpayers never entered into his thinking.

For instance, accepting a little money from Esteban Fernandez to occasionally look the other way, or to send investigators in another direction, was easy money, as far as Senator Thompson was concerned. *Somebody is going to be getting that payoff money. Why shouldn't it be me? I have expenses, after all.*

As Chairman, he had vehemently opposed the contract given to Justice Security. As he had explained to Fernandez, he had done what he could, but he had been outvoted by the other members of the Committee. If he'd had his way, there wouldn't have been *any* government contracts with Justice Security, just to keep the Fernandez money flowing his way. Fernandez would have paid a huge bonus just to keep that from happening.

And now this latest fiasco. Fernandez had been blunt about it.

"Senator, this is your mess. You will clean it up. I've paid you enough money, so you will pay to have it done. If you can't do it, then I will see that someone else assists me with my...*intelligence* needs. Do I make myself clear, *Senor?*"

Thank God for Goodwin and Trammell. They cleaned all of this up for me rather quickly. I don't know how they made the plane explode yesterday, but the bodies were only so much burned mush when the authorities got to the wreckage. Now, if they'd only check in with me! I have one last loose end that needs to be taken care of.

Senator Thompson did not like taking human life, and did it only when he had no other option, or if his way of life were threatened. Letting the cat out of the bag about the payments from Fernandez for sure fell under that heading. If the good voters back home found out about the money he was receiving from Fernandez, they might not understand. They might withhold votes from him, and force him to find another job. He didn't want to do that. He had almost enough money to keep him comfortable down in South America for the rest of his life, but not quite. Just a few more months, and he would announce his retirement, and that would be that.

The fact that he might go to prison if the public found out about the payoffs, or even Trammell and Goodwin's actions to keep things quiet, never occurred to him. That thought was as alien to him as the theory of relativity was to a lab rat. He just couldn't comprehend it.

A quiet knock came from the door of his office.

Thompson stared at the door with an odd look. He didn't have any appointments that he knew of, and his secretary would have buzzed him on the intercom if someone had dropped in.

He took his feet off of the desk, and sat up straight. In his desk drawer, he kept a folder that he used strictly when visitors came to his office. It contained some nonsensical, official-looking papers inside that he used to appear to be working diligently at the duties of a senator of his standing. He took a pen from the holder so that he would appear to be writing. He was ready.

"Come in!" he called.

The door opened. Through it came three men. One was on crutches, with a cast on his leg. The second was a man that was a dead ringer for a young

Tom Selleck. Thompson didn't recognize the third man. Truthfully, he didn't recognize any of them.

Puzzled, he looked at the man on crutches. He seemed to be in charge.

"Good afternoon. May I help you?" Thompson said with some annoyance.

"Yes, Senator, you can," said the man on crutches. "You can help me make a choice."

Still looking puzzled, Thompson smiled lopsidedly. "Sir, I don't understand. Now, I'm a very busy man, and..."

"And you'll help me make this choice, Senator, since it will be one of the last ones you ever make."

"Just who do you think you are, bursting in here and making threats...!"

The man with the crutches interrupted. "My name is Marcus Moore. I have this broken leg because I landed badly when I parachuted out of a plane, and carrying another person that had also jumped." His eyes narrowed. "I'm not happy about it."

"Just what does that have to do with me?"

Ignoring the blustering senator, Marcus continued. "See, the plane I was riding in had been taken over by two gentlemen posing as pilots. To keep from being killed, I had to jump from the plane, along with three other people. We only had two parachutes, and I miscalculated my landing." Marcus sat down heavily in one of the chairs across from Thompson.

Thompson narrowed his eyes as he looked at Marcus. "Marcus Moore? Marcus Moore is dead. He was killed in a plane explosion yesterday."

Marcus smiled. "Not quite. Let me introduce you to these two men. The man that bears the strong resemblance to Tom Selleck is Jim Dandy. The other gentleman is Joey Justice."

The senator looked at Jim. Jim gave him one of his hundred-watt smiles. The senator looked at Joey, and realized that if looks could kill, Joey's would have ripped the senator apart.

"These are two of the people that jumped out of that plane with me yesterday, Senator," continued Marcus. "The third, Misty Wilhite, is waiting in your outer office with several Federal marshals. There are other people that would be delighted to make your acquaintance, like Louie Washington, Jessica Queen, and a lady pilot named Gena Trotter. We've all spent the day at the White House, speaking with both the President and the Attorney General.

We told them our stories, given our sworn statements to a Federal judge, and showed them our evidence." Marcus held up a paper. "They've given me authorization to arrest you for treason, murder, attempted murder, bribery, and whatever else we can come up with."

"No one is arresting anyone..."

Marcus continued, ignoring the interruption. "Or you can choose to issue your resignation to the Vice-President immediately, and be escorted to Guantanamo Bay to be interrogated as to the National Security threat that has been paying you bribes." Marcus leaned close. "That's your choice, Senator. You can choose to go there on your own, or I can arrest you, and put you in general population in a Federal prison until your trial. I can guarantee that you will not be receiving bail, based on evidence that you have several numbered Swiss bank accounts, and would be considered a major flight risk. If you are placed in general population, we will have to hope that Fernandez has no one inside the prison that can get to you before trial. If you survive to your trial, you will be convicted, and will be given either the death penalty, or be expelled to Guantanamo. Either way, Senator, be you dead, or be you alive, you will not be setting foot on U. S. soil again in your lifetime."

Senator Howard Thompson sat frozen, as his stomach dropped to the center of the earth. This was it. His secret was out, and his world was now crumbling. The first thing he thought of was that he wouldn't be playing sex games with eighteen-year-old interns again. His second thought was that his wife would divorce him. The third thing that hit him was that, for all his power, these few people had just stripped away every single shred of it that he had.

The senator abruptly stood, and stated, "I want my lawyer."

Marcus, angered, said, "You'll have access to one after you've been processed into Federal prison for safekeeping."

Joey stared the senator in the eyes. "You almost killed me. You almost killed my two friends. And you almost killed my fiance. I killed one of your men by breaking his neck, and I blew the other one up. And I give you my word, Senator, that as soon as you hit that prison, word will reach Esteban Fernandez that you're telling all you know to the Feds. He will receive that word through some underground associates that know how to pass that word. And those associates will give that word to Fernandez whether you are cooperating or not." Joey was growing angrier by the minute, but he kept his voice at an even level.

"If it were up to me, and I begged the President to let me, I would kill you where you stand. I'll have to settle for one of Fernandez' people doing it for me."

"And, Senator?" said Jim.

Thompson had come out from behind the desk. He stopped and looked at Jim.

"What is it?"

"This is for killing my friend, Michael Brandon." Jim punched the senator in the face with a straight right from the shoulder.

They all watched without sympathy as the formerly most-powerful-senator-in-Washington stood holding his broken nose, and bleeding all over his expensive, vintage Persian rug.

Chapter 18

Jim had incorporated the clients from Jim Dandy Security into Justice Security without effort. Some of his clients were delighted that Jim had joined Justice Security, and were also delighted to receive Justice Security's top-notch service for the same money they had been paying to Jim Dandy Security.

Jim's former employees enjoyed the transfer, too. Many received higher wages, and were delighted with the free medical service provided by Dr. Bishop, the free psychiatric treatment available with Dr. Caleb Mitchell, and the awesome food available in the company cafeteria.

Three days after the meeting in Senator Thompson's office, Marcus called Joey.

"Your word spread quickly. Senator Thompson was stabbed to death in the prison shower. Of course, nobody knows anything."

And no one *really* didn't know anything. They didn't know that it had been a prison guard that did the deed. And they didn't know that the guard had said, "Esteban Fernandez says 'hello'." Nor did they know that it was said just before the knife was plunged into Thompson's neck, severing the jugular.

Lena Marrucci and Tony Armstrong had only the one date. They found themselves struggling to find things to talk about while they had dinner, and both became less enchanted as the night wore on. When they finally came to their good-night kiss, they realized the passion wasn't there. The parting was friendly, however. Lena was receiving training that would allow her to do Tony's job at the new facility.

Emily Owens and Turk Wendell were still a couple. This was a concern to them, since Emily was expected to go with Jim to the new branch office.

Misty had talked to them both about it. "Look, Emily doesn't have to go right away. We're building the new place to be identical to this building, in every way. That means, it has to be built to exacting specifications, and will take time to construct. Jim is going as soon as possible to make sure that no corners are cut. You two will have several months before Emily is needed there. In the meantime, Lena can go with Jim, and help set things up."

In a rare case of bluntness, Emily said, "Oh, *hell*, no! I love Lena, but that little tramp will have Jim so messed up that the top of the building will be on the bottom!" She turned to Turk. "Baby, we'll just have to work around this. We can do it, as long as we keep our love in our hearts. Okay, baby?"

Turk grunted his agreement.

Joey and Dexter were talking to Jim about the new building.

"What I plan is to set things up so that all of our systems can be switched to the new place with only one or two buttons being pushed," Dexter was saying. "If we ever have to abandon this building, or disappear for a while, we'll have to make sure that we have everything that we have here."

Jim nodded. "Sound great to me. What do you want me to do when I get there?"

Joey shrugged. "Well, construction starts very soon. They're starting from scratch, so the hole for the six floors below ground will be the first thing that the company does. You'll need to oversee the entire thing. You have to make sure that they're into bedrock underneath, make sure that they lay the foundation properly...everything, Jim. It's all going to be on you for now."

"Yeah, we'll come visit every so often and help you out. But it's six hours away, so it won't be that often," added Dexter.

"The biggest thing to keep in mind, and you'll need to drill it into Emily and Lena, too, is that this is *secret*. The locals are not to know, and that includes law enforcement, city and county officials, Joe Blow on the street...*no*-body can know what that building is, or our little secret bolt-hole will be useless. At least, for hiding in, anyway."

Jim nodded. "Understood."

"And you'll have Patty and Brandon to help you, too. They're good, Jim. They're very good."

Dexter said, "Oh, and that reminds me, Joey. The kids asked for a couple of weeks off, and I gave it to them. Patty wanted to go back out to Nevada for a while, and Brandon is tagging along, too. I think he wants to try to double that money he won."

Joey and Jim laughed. The story of the dollar machine had spread all through the company, and the kids were still the subject of admiration, jokes, and general good feelings for them for their win.

He waved his hand. "That's fine with me. Let them have some fun. They've earned it." He turned back to Jim. "Our legal people have made sure that all of the proper permits have been taken out, and that no one knows what the building is going to be, or who actually owns it. They also rented some apartment in that town for you five. Those will be your homes until the building is complete. After that, you guys will live in the building itself."

Joey looked at Dexter. "Can you think of anything else?"

Dexter thought for a moment, and then shook his head.

"Okay, Jim, that's it. Welcome back! And say a little prayer that we find a way to get this other person to accept a partnership."

Jim smiled at his friend. "I'll be praying for an angel to intervene!"

YOU'RE READY FOR BOOK 10 in the *Justice Security* series: *Cow Patty – A Justice Security Novel.*

It's available at your favorite eBook seller.

About The Author: T. M. Bilderback is a former radio announcer with a number of story ideas running around inside his head, most based on, or inspired by, classic songs. The author currently resides in Tennessee, and is writing feverishly in order to banish these stories from his head and into book form, before they drive him screaming into the street.

Other works by T. M. Bilderback
Nicholas Turner
If You Could Read My Mind
Justice Security
Mama Told Me Not To Come
Someone Saved My Life Tonight
Jackie Blue
Wake Me Up Before You Go-Go
Saturday In The Park
MacArthur Park
The Little Drummer Boy
The Night Chicago Died
Jim Dandy
Cow Patty
Hell's Bells
Tales Of Sardis County
Don't Come Around Here No More
Junior's Farm
The Devil's In The Details
I'm Your Boogie Man
Colonel Abernathy's Tales
The Lion Sleeps Tonight
Heart Of Glass
Other Stories
The Wreck Of The Edmund Fitzgerald
Gold
Hot Child In The City
Eli's Coming
Other Novels
Empty Eyes
Story Collections
Greatest Hits

www.ingramcontent.com/pod-product-compliance
Lightning Source LLC
Chambersburg PA
CBHW031128210626
46816CB00015B/1183